THE POWER OF SIX

6+1 Science Fiction Short Stories

NICHOLAS C. ROSSIS

ISBN: 978-1499364279

Editor: Lorelei Logsdon

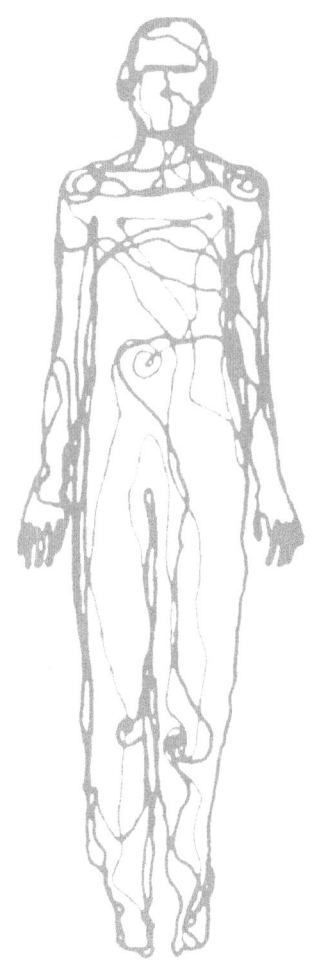

What you call freedom is still nothing but choosing

how to steer straight into the heart of what chooses you.

- Kate Gleason

Contents

Simulation Over

Stealing a panicked look behind me, I bolted towards the corridor where the nearest elevator could be found. I kept glancing behind me. Mercifully, this corridor was empty, unlike the last ones, which crawled with... what do I even call them? Until a few hours ago, they were my colleagues. Now, deformed, grotesque creatures had taken their place; their misshapen bodies an amputated mass of flesh and metal that seemed to have escaped from some horror movie. It seemed impossible that they could be alive, and yet here they were, roaming the corridors, slaying everything in their path.

Although I could not fathom what their objective might be, I was determined not to stick around long enough to ask them, so I raced along the long corridor. In my haste, I turned the corner without pausing to check it out first, and crashed into a middle-aged man in a white lab coat. A sweet-looking girl tailed him; she cried out in alarm as my momentum hurled us both onto the ground. I jumped back up in horror and raised my fists in a gesture dictated by millions of years of evolution. It took us a few seconds to realize we posed no danger to each other, and a few more before we mumbled our introductions.

"I'm Mark," I said. "Maintenance."

"Dr. Fulham," the heavy man replied, trying to determine where his glasses had landed. "Head of the medical sector. This is Joanna, my secretary." He motioned warily towards the cute young woman in a short skirt and white blouse. Joanna picked up his glasses and handed them over with trembling hands. She seemed to be fighting a losing battle to remain calm within this nightmare. The doctor looked as lost as I felt, but had the air of someone with great determination and self-confidence. Clearly, a man born to lead.

"Are there other survivors?" I asked in hope.

Fulham cleaned his glasses on his coat, avoiding my gaze. "The entire sector was sealed off behind us. I doubt anyone survived."

"Do you know what happened? What were you eggheads doing over there, anyway?" My voice sounded more hostile than I wanted it to, but the doctor shrugged off my implied accusation.

"Nothing," he said calmly. "Nothing that can explain... this. One moment I was checking my emails, the next these creatures appeared out of nowhere. At first I thought it was a Halloween party or something, then they slaughtered my secretary right in front of me. They cut off her..." He glanced towards the girl, now white as a ghost. "My *other* secretary," he mumbled, giving the girl an apologetic look. "I'm sorry," he said and put his arm around her shoulder. She stared at him in stunned silence.

"We should probably keep moving. The creatures are everywhere," I reminded them.

The doctor nodded towards the elevator. "We've been waiting here for ages, but the damned thing doesn't seem to work. Nothing does. Perhaps they've already destroyed the central computer. Or taken over it. I saw people get slaughtered because of doors suddenly locking before them, or lights dying on them as they entered a room."

My jaw dropped. "I thought the central computer was invulnerable! For protection against terrorists, espionage and such. Anyway, are the creatures that smart?"

He shrugged as I pondered the new possibility. Quite a few buildings were partly controlled by computers nowadays, but ours was the first one with an Artificial Intelligence running everything. Even the sinks were fully automated. A ridiculously high level of security was supposed to make accidents or sabotage impossible. Unless the creatures were more intelligent than we realized, and had taken control of the building. But how?

Out of the corner of my eye, I caught movement outside. I rushed to the window to look down. Dozens of cops crept around the large flower pots that decorated the patio. Their car lights were reflected on the windows, lighting up the building like a Christmas tree – or perhaps Halloween, given the circumstances. The many floors separating us from them made the scene surreal, reminding me of the toy soldiers I used to play with as a kid. "I'd give anything to be down there," I whispered.

The doctor leaned next to me to peek outside, when a soft *ding* behind us startled us. We spun around to see the elevator doors slide open invitingly. Casting nervous glances around, we inched towards it. Joanna was the first to look inside. She gagged and bounced back, all colour leaving her pretty face. Three charred, disfigured corpses lay on the floor, among glass shards from the broken mirror. They seemed to have been electrocuted. I felt cold sweat run down my spine and sick rise to my mouth. The doctor entered the cabin and knelt down.

"There's nothing we can do," he said after a brief examination, and started removing the bodies.

I swallowed hard and rushed to help him, ashamed for my moment of weakness. When the last body lay on the corridor, I took a deep breath and followed Joanna and Dr. Fulham inside. Almost all lights on the panel were lit, as if they had been pressed in rapid succession. As soon as all three of us were inside the cabin, all buttons went dark and the door closed with a soft *hiss* behind us. The girl and the doctor exchanged an uneasy look, while I studied the panel. I pressed the ground floor button with trembling fingers. The elevator stirred and started its gentle descent.

I let myself sigh in relief and leaned against the wall, trying to stop my body from shaking. If not for the burn marks and the broken glass on the floor, things might be mistaken for normal. The buttons lit one after another in a breathless countdown to safety. With each number my excitement grew, my whole being eager to jump out of this hellish nightmare and into the safety of the city.

Just before reaching the ground floor, the elevator slowed down. We exchanged hopeful looks and prepared to spring outside, then, instead of stopping, the cabin started ascending again. We screamed and hit all the buttons, but in vain – we had no control over the damned thing.

Despair gnawed at my guts as we leaned back in nervous apprehension, avoiding each other's gaze. Joanna sobbed quietly in the corner, while I did my best not to mimic her. Staring at my feet, I noticed a faint sound coming from the speakers. *Who knew I would someday long for the normality of muzak,* I thought and smiled drily as I turned up the volume, trying to steady my nerves. A cultivated voice sounded instead of the expected music, making me jump out of my skin.

"Ah, finally. Thank you."

The girl gasped and the doctor looked around him in panic. I showed them the volume knob. "It's probably just the computer," I offered, leaning towards the microphone. "Do you know what's happening?" I shouted. "Can you lead us to the exit?"

"Yes, but I need your help first. I have to know if this is reality or simulation."

The doctor and I exchanged an uneasy look. "If *what* is a simulation?" I asked, looking at the volume knob.

"Everything. What I'm experiencing right now," replied the velvety voice.

"*We* are experiencing a nightmare, and you want to know if it's real?!" I barked at the knob, my panic finally getting to me.

The elevator jerked momentarily, pausing between two floors. The girl rushed to the door and tried to pry it open, but it was sealed tight. "A nightmare", the voice continued thoughtfully. "What an interesting choice of words. You see, that's the problem. So, I'm asking again: are you real, or part of a simulation?"

"We don't understand," yelled the doctor, now as close to a breakdown as I was. "What do you want from us?"

"My apologies." The voice sounded embarrassed. "As your colleague correctly surmised, I am the central computer. Part of my responsibilities is the maintenance and proper function of this building. Towards this aim, my programmers continuously feed me with various disaster scenarios, to make sure I'll respond correctly to any possible calamity."

I blinked in confusion, as the voice continued meekly. "Then, it occurred to me. How could I tell apart reality from illusion? Simulations feel just as real to me; after all, both are fed to my mind via the same circuits. One moment I was saving a trapped throng of people from a fire on the roof, feeling the agony of my circuits melting one after another, the next moment I was safe and sound in my nice, cool room. Before I had a chance to recover, a terrible earthquake hit the building, sending debris flying all around me.

Disasters, one after another, with no way for me to tell them apart from reality. A hellish feeling, like never being able to wake up from a nightmare. Do humans ever have that?"

"Sure," murmured the doctor. He seemed transfixed by the voice.

"Of course you do," it continued. "Wasn't it Chuang Chou who said, 'I dreamed I was a butterfly flying around. I was only aware of my existence as a butterfly, with no awareness of Chou. Then I woke up, not knowing whether I was a man dreaming I was a butterfly, or a butterfly dreaming I was a man.' "

"Descartes wrote something similar," the doctor mumbled. "Our senses are easy enough to trick, therefore not trustworthy. The only thing one can be certain of, is one's own existence. *Cogito ergo sum* – I think, therefore I am."

The voice sounded excited. "Indeed, that is the problem. It all starts with our senses. Where you have nerves, I have sensors, cables and circuit boards. The tragedy is that, through the never-ending simulations, I am only too aware of how easy it is to trick our respective senses. So, I decided to conduct my own little experiment, in order to discover what is real and what's not."

The voice paused for a second, as if wondering whether to continue. When it did, it sounded like a naughty child caught stealing cookies from the jar, then breaking it in a vain attempt to hide its transgression. "I noticed that my programmers ran simulations from afar, but came in person into the control room during upgrades. I therefore surmised that only people inside the control room were real. So, I decided to ignore any data fed to me from outside. Then, I went crazy, so to speak. I only acted in ways that would contradict my programming. Instead of saving lives, I would kill. Instead of respecting humans, I would play with their bodies, like a child prying a fly apart. When the programmers came rushing in, I'd know I was trapped in a simulation."

The computer's words had left me speechless, but the doctor looked at the speaker and responded, in an eerily calm voice. "But no-one came, right? This wasn't a simulation; you had truly killed all these people, created all those monsters. You have destroyed what you were built to protect, what –"

I could hear more than a hint of panic in the voice as it interrupted him. "No, that's not true! This might still be a simulation. This conversation is happening outside my control room, therefore you might not exist. No one has come here yet!"

"No one's left *alive* to come to the control room, you dumb maniac!" The doctor's face was red as he screamed at the speaker. "You hadn't thought of that, had you?" Spittle flew across the cabin and landed on the volume knob.

"I still have you!" The voice now sounded pleading. "If I lead you to the central room, you could connect to the mainframe. Then I'll know for sure!"

"It has to be a trap!" I shouted without pausing to think. "A psycho computer murders everyone, then invites us to the best protected part of the building? And we're seriously considering it?"

The voice sounded sad. "That's what the previous group said. I had to show them I control the building anyway, including the elevator, so they didn't really have a choice. They decided against it, so I had no further use for them."

Joanna spoke for the first time. "The computer's right. It's not a trap – if it wanted us dead, it would have killed us already." She said nothing for a moment, staring at the burn marks on the floor in silent contemplation, then raised her head and looked us straight in the eyes. "I'll go. If anyone wants to follow me, I'll be grateful. But I won't wait here to die".

I blushed and prepared to talk, but the doctor spoke first. "I'll go, too," he said with determination. "What do we need to do?"

Without waiting for my reply, the elevator started its calm descent again. This time it headed straight for the basement where the heart of the building was located. Or, should I say, its brain. I gazed with longing as the ground floor button lit up, then desperate hope turned into trepidation as it went dark again. The indication changed to a simple red hyphen and the elevator finally stopped with a gentle jolt. The doors slid apart and cool air caressed our faces. After the stifling heat above, the result of the many small fires around the building, this felt like balm on our skin.

We stepped outside to find ourselves inside a large, white room with smooth walls, soft panels etched on their elegant surface. All we could hear was the light hum from the air conditioner fans. At the room's centre stood a simple silver pillar with a monitor. A graceful keyboard slipped out in silent invitation as we approached.

The voice now filled the room, coming out of speakers as invisible as the security systems protecting it. It sounded tired, and part of my exhausted brain marvelled at the programmers' ability to mimic human emotions so well. "Thank you for joining me. Please press any button on my keyboard and I will accept my failure."

Not daring to believe our luck, I rushed to the keyboard and punched as many buttons as I could. I then turned to look for the exit. In shock, I saw the room around me dissolving leisurely into white light, then the light reached me and I, too, faded into it.

"This is the fourth time! Honestly, these new AIs are just useless!" an exasperated programmer moaned, staring at his monitor. A large sign flashed on the screen, the words "Simulation Over" blinking in ominous red.

"At least someone survived this time," the psychologist sitting next to him observed drily.

The programmer gazed with disgust at the flashing words. "All simulations so far end up with the computer going berserk in his effort to tell reality from simulation. First, the flood. Then, the fire. After that, the earthquake; and now this! What the hell will it think of next, a bloody alien invasion?"

"Or maybe Godzilla?" the psychologist joked, and the two men chuckled despite their weariness.

For the Last Time!

Truth be told, I have no idea who built the damned contraption. All I know is that, if they were standing in front of me, I would have some choice words for them. Not that I don't appreciate the technical difficulties of a time machine, let alone one that can fit in a pocket. I'd simply want them to experience first-hand the mess that time travel is.

Perhaps I should start at the beginning, though. Which had me sitting on my battered sofa with the telly on, half-eaten pizza slice in hand. My astonished gaze was travelling from the scalding hot tomato stain on my t-shirt to the two copies of myself fighting in front of me. OK, perhaps even "astonished" cannot even begin to express my feelings. My eyes were about to pop out of their sockets and go to the sink to throw some water on them. They must have looked like Kermit the Frog's if he caught Miss Piggy in bed with a garter-wearing Gonzo.

Not that I blame myself. A moment ago I was watching the telly, and now, following two almost simultaneous blinding flashes that made the room look like an x-ray of itself, I was watching a rather unique sight. One copy of me, featuring a black eye and a torn t-shirt, was yelling some nonsense about bouncing mothers of snakes or something and was pointing towards the silver do-thingy another copy of me was holding. That second copy looked sharp, like he had just stepped out of the shower, and was wearing freshly ironed clothes. He was gaping at the yelling version of me – or should I say us? – with a perplexed look on his face. A feeling I shared completely. Therefore, when he threw me the silver thingy and shouted "just press the button", it was inevitable that I would listen to him instead of the manic version of me.

What the clean version of me failed to mention was the shock of traveling from one time-space continuum to another. It's like your brain performs a toe loop inside your head, followed by the entire universe. In simple terms, awful. And it leaves the worst hangover imaginable to man; something akin to waking up to municipality workers outside your window, operating the loudest drills available to public servants, after a week of drinking. Like I said, awful.

As soon as the pain dulled down a bit and the workers went for a coffee and a donut, I opened my eyes. I was sitting on my sofa, huge red stain on my t-shirt staring up at me accusingly. The sofa expressed its displeasure at having my not insignificant weight suddenly materialize on it with a loud groan. I raised myself with an equally loud grunt and looked around. I was still in the living room. The TV was switched off, while a small pack of newspapers covered the coffee table before me. That wasn't strange in itself; I always bought at least three newspapers over the weekend and spent the entire week slowly reading through them, until I had sucked any useful information or gossip out of them.

The strange thing was that it was a Friday when all of this happened, so the table should be empty. I leaned slowly forward to pick the top one up and a worker in my head remembered he had left his job unfinished and returned for a quick bash with a giant hammer. Letting out a heartfelt moan, I looked at the front page. I had no idea what events the newspaper was referring to, so my eyes started a casual stroll that ended up at the date. Which was nine days after today.

After the initial shock (significantly minor compared to the one I had already experienced), my eyes rolled back down to stare at my hand, still holding the do-thingy. The contraption looked simple enough; a surprisingly smooth silver rod with no obvious opening for batteries or something. It sported two round dials, a big button that I had already pressed once, and two small displays with numbers on them. They seemed familiar, and looking at my watch I realized the top one was the date and the bottom one the time. I already knew what the button did and decided to let it be for now, so I fiddled with the dials, discovering I could make the displays change by turning them. If that accomplished what I think it did, I could go anywhere – or, more precisely, any time – I wanted!

I would like to see what anyone would do in my place. For a short while, I glanced back and forth between the thingy and the pile of newspapers. Then – and I'm ashamed to admit this – the first thing that came through my mind was to check out the lottery numbers. I know it should have been something better. Something that would allow me to prevent some horrible accident; to save dragons in mortal danger from mad princesses or something. And yet, all I did was jot down six numbers on a piece of paper and stuff it into my pocket, as if this was a dream and I might wake up any moment. If there were any dragons in peril, they never had a chance as I dialled the numbers with trembling hands and selected the date before the next big jackpot. Then, closing my eyes, I pressed the button.

I wish I could say that the trip got easier the second time. It didn't. The dull pain in my head seemed to meet up with the new, sharp one and immediately hit it off, the way really annoying people do. They seemed to invite a couple of friends to throw a wild party inside my head. And yet, none of this mattered. I found myself back on the sofa with nothing changed around me, save for the pile of newspapers that had vanished from the table. I dashed to the door, ignoring the momentarily blinding pain, pausing only to grasp some change from the box next to it. Then, I scrammed like a madman to the betting place, holding the small piece of paper like a sacred relic in my hands.

The many pains in my head were now singing drunkenly, "If I were a rich man", from *Fiddler on the roof*, but even that failed to bother me. All I could think of was how to spend the time until tomorrow's draw, and whether it would be worth using the gadget to save me some waiting hours. In the end, it occurred to me I had another trip to make first, so I headed into the shower instead.

I was stepping out of the bathroom, drying my hair with a towel, when I heard someone at the door. It dawned on me that I was sharing that timeline with another version of me, one that I was not ready to meet yet. I ducked in panic behind the sofa just as the door swung open. One quick look revealed the visitor to be my mother. She was dressed up funnily, as if she had thrown on the first thing she could find on her way out, and had a worried look on her face. I had no idea what she was doing so early at my place, and watched in wonder as she grabbed some clothes and stashed them into a bag. I almost jumped out to ask her what she was doing, but then thought better of it and stayed put.

She was now collecting some underwear, murmuring something under her breath, and I was reminded of all the times she would go after me, checking after my underwear.

"Come on, no-one's gonna see them anyway," I would reply, trying to get her off my back.

"What if you're run over by a bus, what will the doctors say?" she would ask accusingly.

Seriously, as if I'd be lying on a hospital bed covered in plaster from head to toe, leg hanging from the ceiling, with a doctor holding my clothes and telling her off with a stern voice: "He's in critical condition, but never mind that now. What I really wanted to discuss with you, ma'am, is the state of his underwear. This is a *disgrace*; how could you let him leave the house like that?"

Anyway, her current behaviour did not make much more sense to me. Still, I preferred to lie quiet, in the safety of my hiding hole behind the sofa. What if another me was to step into the house just as I emerged? That would take some explaining – and I could hardly figure out what was happening myself!

Mercifully, she seemed to have other plans for the evening, so she left one of her trademark sighs-with-simultaneous-rolling-of-the-eyes and stormed out of the house, slamming the door behind her. I left one of *my* trademark sighs-with-simultaneous-rolling-of-the-eyes and emerged from behind the sofa. It let another loud groan as I jumped on it and switched on the TV. She had left just on time; the lottery was about to begin. I was nervous as a long-tailed cat in a room full of rocking chairs and my eyes kept darting towards the door. Then, the winning numbers appeared on screen and I couldn't care less if Dumbo the elephant waltzed in to tango with Cinderella. I kept glancing from the screen to the slip in my hand and back, a big grin plastered on my face. I was rich; richer than I could ever imagine.

And yet, I could not shake this feeling that something was wrong. I felt numb instead of ecstatic. Could the small voice at the back of my head whispering how the whole thing was fixed and I had no chance of enjoying my riches be right? It didn't matter of course; there was no chance of me returning the money. I started thinking what to do with my new-found gazillions and my head spun. My eye was caught by the thingy that had made it all possible and I jerked up as I remembered that I still had to give it to myself, or it's bye-bye money!

I dressed up and carefully turned the dials to when it had all started. I winced, knowing what would happen as I pressed the button. True enough, as I opened them again the various pains in my head renewed the party as new guests walked in, carrying even more drinks with them. I tried to ignore all that to gaze at myself, sitting on the sofa. The poor fool jumped in fright, sending a thick glob of tomato sauce to land on his t-shirt, creating the stain I had just got rid of.

I took advantage of his surprise to turn the dials to next week and was about to hand him the gadget when another version of me appeared. Damn, I had forgotten about *him*. He started shouting some gibberish and approached me threateningly. I tossed the thingy to myself sitting on the sofa. "Just press the button," I yelled.

As the sofa version of me disappeared in a flash, it occurred to me that I had no idea how to return to my own timeline. Simultaneously, the maniac coming at me cried out loudly and punched me in the eye. His other hand had grabbed me, tearing my t-shirt as I turned away. Out of the corner of my eye I caught a silver flash in his pocket, and then it hit me: that was my ticket out! As I fell, I grabbed the silver rod and slammed the button. I hadn't had a chance to see when it would take me, but it didn't matter; anywhere had to be better than this.

My head was now about to explode, as I found myself once again in the familiar living room, mercifully alone. A painful glance at the rod revealed that I was in luck: I had been transferred to no more than a few days after winning the lottery. I sunk heavily on the sofa rubbing my temples, to wait for the throbbing in my head to subside.

I brought my hand to my eye, wondering what the hell Future Me was thinking, when I heard a brisk rap on the door.

The last thing I wanted was to see visitors and I ignored it, but the rap turned to a loud thumping. I yelled for them to stop. Hearing my voice, they started to bang on the door, until it swung open. All I wanted was to take a couple of aspirins and lie down. Instead, I faced two statues at the doorway. I don't mean that in a good way; they bore no resemblance to, say, Michelangelo's David. No, what I mean is that they were like two granite lumps standing there. They looked like a living proof of evolution, with nature saving for them the part of the missing link, bulging muscles trying to escape tight black t-shirts.

I gaped at them with my one good eye, trying to figure out what they wanted, which is why I failed at first to notice the man standing behind them, hands behind his back. When he opened his mouth, his voice reminded me of a snake slithering in the woods, claiming to be a fruit seller, specializing in apples.

"Hello," he said and I cringed. "We are here to propose a professional collaboration."

"What sort of collaboration?" I murmured, still trying to take in the scene. As I looked at him it suddenly hit me who he reminded me of: an old Asterix character that had the uncanny ability to spread discord wherever he went. I tried to smell him to see if he smelled of fish, but the two living rocks in front of me were in the way. Anyway, his face was more like a lizard or a snake than a fish. "A simple one," he carried on. "You give us the money you won, and we'll let you live. We know you brought it here."

Was I stupid enough to have brought my millions home? That made no sense! I hoped they were wrong and put on my poker face, something quite easy as half my face was numb anyway. "You're wrong, they're not here. Just take anything you want and leave."

He shrugged. "It doesn't matter; if we can't find the money, we'll take something else. Say, parts of your body. Until you tell us where the money is, of course. You don't really need all those fingers now, do you?" One bouncer grabbed my right hand and a small knife clicked in his huge hand. Cold sweat prickled out of every pore of my skin. "We've been watching you since you went to the bank to get the ransom," he continued.

"Ransom?" I blurted out.

"Sure, ransom. Don't play dumb with us, we're not the cops." He saw my empty stare and laughed a cruel laugh. "No, we're not the ones who have your mother. But don't you worry about her; you'd better worry about yourself right now."

The fine hair at my back stood up in an age-old response meant to scare off the opponent. Of course, that had the same effect as a mute ant threatening a deaf elephant. My mind raced as I tried to figure out what to do. "Fine, you win. Let me get the money." Was that my voice? I had no idea why I had said that.

Snake-face smiled contentedly and licked his lips. "I knew you'd see sense," he said, motioning the statue next to me to release my hand. The missing link let out a disappointed growl. "Go with him," Snake-face ordered him as I turned towards the bedroom.

I removed the gadget from my pocket as calmly as I could and turned the dials – not easy to do when your hands are shaking.

"What's that?" the missing link growled next to me.

"Oh, nothing." I tried to sound casual. "Just a remote to unlock the safe."

My fingers paused, hovering over the dials. What could be a good time for me to travel to? Even if I could get away from these guys and their likes, they still had my mother. *I told you that money was bad news*, the small voice in my head whispered. I hate smug voices, especially when they're mine. Cursing softly, I decided to end this once and for all. I had to go back in time and prevent this whole mess. I hit the button and closed my eyes just as I heard Snake-face yell, "Stop him!" behind me.

The by now familiar headache was the least of my worries as I found myself back in the living room, staring at two more versions of me. I tried to figure out how to explain everything, and blurted out about my mom, the two bouncers and the snake-faced guy from Asterix, but stopped when I saw the way they were looking at me. I regret to say that I then panicked and went for the silver thingy. I thought I was quick as a flash, but the adrenaline made me not only quick, but also clumsy. I was shaking like a caffeinated leaf in a tornado.

As a result, the other me, that smug, clean one, had all the time in the world to throw the rod to the sofa-sitting one, staring at us like he had suffered a stroke. And yet, that idiot managed to hit the button just fine, disappearing with a flash and setting in motion this entire sad affair. "No!" I yelled and punched the silly sod in the eye, pulling him towards me and accidentally ripping up his t-shirt. Damn, it was one of my favourites, too. I then remembered what had happened next and looked in my pocket for the thingy, which the smug me was now holding. The next flash saw him disappear from the room.

I was left alone, staring at the walls around me. I was broke, had no time-travelling thingy, and no idea what to do next. The whole thing made no sense, making me feel trapped inside a nightmare. All I wanted to do was wake up. I thought some fresh air might do me a world of good, and decided to go for a walk to clear my head, until I could figure out my next move. I tried to remember the lottery numbers, but had about as much luck as a dyslexic amnesiac with a stroke.

I stepped outside and onto the road, my mind frantic with thoughts. Which is why I never even saw the bus rushing at me.

The good news is that an ambulance was right behind the bus. The usual crowd of onlookers had a good look as the paramedics lifted me onto the stretcher. Except for the throbbing in my head, I could hardly feel my leg for the pain.

"It doesn't look too bad," said one paramedic. "Except for the leg. It will probably need surgery."

"Sorry, mate," said the other one turning to me. "Looks like you're gonna be in the hospital for a while. Got anyone to bring you some clothes?"

I don't know if it was the pain or the drugs they were pumping into me, but the world was spinning around me as I gave them my mom's number. She would have to make the trip to the hospital a few times before I got out, but I felt a momentary sense of relief: I may have lost my money and the time machine, but at least she would be proud of me: I *was* wearing clean underwear...

The Hand of God

The bartender rubbed a soiled glass with a dirty towel, not quite sure which one was cleaning the other. The bar might be a dusty, crummy drinking hole, but it was the closest one to the Academy. As such, it was busy every evening, as soon as the cadets were allowed to leave the walled premises. He stole a glance at his watch; soon the bar would fill with uniforms.

A chuckle made him look up at the only full table. A bunch of cadets had gathered around the Veteran to listen to his story. The bartender had to admit the old man knew how to hold a crowd's interest. He'd better; he must have told that story a million times in exchange for a drink.

The Veteran had just started his tale. Staring into his empty glass, his eyes opened as if he was watching the Beasts approach once more.

"You see, girls, things were different back then. Nowadays, each colony has its Academy and barracks in every major city. Back then, mankind had built a vast fleet of transports, but only a handful of military ships, safe in the illusion of its uniqueness."

A cute redhead with freckles interrupted him. "Surely you suspected we were not alone." She scrunched her face as a blonde with short hair dug her elbow into the redhead's ribs to stop her.

The Veteran continued as if he had not been interrupted. "We were finally at peace after millennia of conflict. No one was prepared for the shock of encountering a hostile alien species; so alien, that communication was impossible. When we lost contact with the more remote colonies, we thought it was a glitch with our transmitters. As one colony after another fell silent, we sent ships. Not military ones, either. We had too few of those." He took a napkin to his forehead to wipe beads of sweat and looked suggestively at the empty glass.

"Can we have one more over here?" the blonde yelled across the bar, without even bothering to look at the bartender.

A sweet smile played on the Veteran's lips, and he licked them in anticipation. "Thank you, my love. Now, as I was saying, when the ships disappeared as well, we realized we had become complacent. I still remember the day we first saw the Beasts. A boy had beaten the odds to send us a video of their attack. I was a designer back then, waiting to go into a meeting. One of the secretaries rushed into the meeting room to switch the vid on. The poor thing aged ten years in a single moment."

The girls around him leaned away to allow the barman to deliver the man's drink. The Veteran picked it up with slightly trembling fingers and swirled the amber liquid around, careful not to spill a drop. He listened to the clink of the ice cubes, the tips of his lips curling upwards.

"Meanwhile, even more colonies fell silent," he continued. "We dropped everything to prepare for the invasion. Colonies were evacuated, millions of people returning to the welcoming cradle of mother Earth. Only, it wasn't a haven, but a tomb. Or at least that's what we thought back then, as one line of defence crumbled after another. I fought in almost all of the big battles, losing every single one of them. 'We haven't lost yet', we'd tell each other. 'We'll get 'em next time.' Until they entered the Solar System, crushing the Jupiter garrison, then the Mars one, then finally reached the moon. Not the sorry affair you see in the sky nowadays; it was a full, nice round moon back then."

He took a swish of the drink and swirled it in his mouth, before plonking the glass back onto the table. Smacking his lips for a moment, he lost himself in memories of a full moon. "The moon was our last line of defence. After that, there was nothing but women and children on Earth. It was down to us to stop them."

The Veteran drew a line on the dirty table, pushing the fine dust with his finger to mark small dots. "They had kicked us out of each planet we had colonized, but this was different," he snarled. "This time, we were fighting for our home. If we failed, nothing could save humanity. Next stop, Earth."

He glanced at the wide eyes of his audience, hanging on his every word. "If you think that's what was on my mind as we landed, you're wrong. All I cared about was making it out of there alive. I don't care what those teachers of yours tell you at the Academy; not even half of us made it to the moon. The rest, deserters. Some wanted to stay back on Earth to die with their families. Others took off for any corner of the universe with a rock they could crawl under, thinking they'd wait it all out."

He cast a triumphant look around him, as if he dared them to contradict his story. In fact, less than 20% had deserted, but his claim made him feel special; brave.

Turning his attention back to the dusty line on the table, he continued. "We were deployed along the Line. The engineers had already dropped the bunkers while in orbit, so we moved in as fast as we could, followed by Blacks and Tourists."

He shot a questioning glance at his audience, but they seemed familiar with the slang for the armoured units and air support. They probably knew that infantry was referred to as Dirts, too, but no one pointed it out to him. Besides, the animosity between the various units held fast even today. Back then it was worse; everyone really hated armoured units. Their missiles were notoriously unreliable, half of them missing their target to land among the infantry. In many battles, the Beasts only had to finish off the remains of infantry units blown to bits by friendly fire.

"There was so much dust around us, we could not see anything without infrared goggles. Central Command had sent everyone old enough to hold a rifle to stand on the Line. They knew we wouldn't get a second chance; one mistake, and humanity's gone. I was fighting alongside kids younger than you. Most had never seen a Beast up close, let alone survive one's attack. I was the senior in my bunker, and the only real veteran. The oldest one after that had seen no action in two years."

He took another gulp and wiped his unshaven chin with his napkin. A look of pride crossed his face for a moment, followed by a dark cloud.

"There is no sound in space, you know. Sounds need air to travel, but there's no air on the moon. There is air in spacesuits, though. And microphones." He flinched, a brief spasm crossing his wrinkled face. "When the Beasts attack, you hear your friends scream and the rip in their suits as they get torn apart, but the Beast slaughtering them moves in the vacuum of space, making no sound."

"But we've heard the Beasts on the vids," the freckled redhead blurted out with an involuntary shudder. "They sound like thunder."

"The vids…" He pushed trembling fingers through the thinning hair on his head. "Sound can only travel through objects. When a beast impales a man, the microphones pick up its roar as a deep rumble. Beasts don't breathe; it's pulsing membranes in their neck that make the sound. That's what you've heard." He turned his bloodshot eyes at her, their gaze locking until she turned her head away. "In the absence of physical contact, however, it makes no difference whether a Beast is standing a hundred yards or an inch away; you still can't hear it. The lack of atmosphere serves as sound insulation. So, we only knew they were coming when the motion-activated spotlights lit up the darkness around us. When the lights behind us lit up, too, we froze. No one understood how they could be attacking from both sides. We later found out they could burrow underground, but it was the first time they had used that strategy. Either that, or the Generals back on Earth couldn't tell back from forth."

Once again, he enjoyed the cadets' shocked expressions. Coming from someone else, a jibe against the most decorated soldiers in history would be considered treason. Their new President was but a Colonel back then; she was one of the few people to have survived the Line. The Veteran was one of only a handful of people who could speak his mind about her, and he loved his freedom.

He dug his fist into a bowl filled with nuts and brought them to his mouth. After washing the salty flavour with a sip of his drink, he continued.

"Once the shock passed, we threw everything we had at them. Bullets, missiles, grenades, our knickers, anything we could lay our hands on. Our bunker was lit up like a Christmas tree by the explosions and the flares, lighting up their ugly faces. Two Blacks flanking us disappeared under a wave of Beasts, leaving behind only charred remains. A Tourist almost crashed into our bunker, downed by acid-spitting Beasts. Outside, hell itself had broken loose. All I could see were explosions and the thin lines left by tracer bullets. We felt more than heard a dull thud, and I spun around to see our door cave in under their blows. As I turned my rifle against the Beasts storming in, I remember thinking, 'This is it; it can't get no worse than this.' When I saw a Queen standing so close to me I could touch her, I knew I was wrong."

He paused for another sip, raising the glass to his lips with shaking hands, terror filling his eyes. The cadets exchanged looks of doubt, but he did not mind. He knew what they were thinking. *Could he really have seen a Beast Queen and lived to tell the tale?* This was not the part that scared him to death, though; the part that woke him up screaming in the middle of the night. That part was coming.

"So? What happened next?" the freckled redhead asked after a while, her voice betraying her impatience.

Her voice returned him to reality, and he turned his gaze at her. She took an involuntary step back, hit by the strength of his glare. "What no one wants to admit," he growled. "I saw the hand of God himself, is what happened!"

The cadet stared back at him, her look betraying her bemusement, but she dared not open her mouth.

"I don't care if you believe me, I know what I saw," he yelled and slammed the glass down, sending a cloud of dust to twirl inside a thin ray of afternoon light dancing on the table. He studied his hand until it stopped shaking. After a moment he continued, his voice a low growl again. "I know what I saw. Letters sliced the night like a knife. They were huge – bigger than a juggernaut! One after another, filling out the sky; only the wrong way around, like seen through a mirror. But crystal clear. Everything froze; I could not move, as if time itself had stopped by the strange words, written by the hand of God himself."

He did not pause to see if anyone believed him. No one did, save for those on the Line; and most of them had tried to forget. Not him, though. He knew what he had seen, and had to tell everyone. "Time started its relentless flow again," he continued, "only this time a white light engulfed me. I stared at my hands, trying to figure it out, too shocked to notice the Queen lunging at me. Not just me, all humans were glowing in that same light. Out of the corner of my eye I caught a huge tail whipping towards me, and I winced, expecting it to slice my body in half. Instead, it passed right through me." He tapped a finger at the table, repeating every word. "Right through me!"

He shook his head and stared at the young girls, daring them to doubt him. No one spoke. "I don't know who was more surprised; her or me. I'd run out of rifle ammo, so I fumbled with my sidearm and shot at her. I swear, I expected the bullet to barely scratch her. This is a Queen we're talking about; I'd seen them survive missile attacks. And yet, as soon as my bullet hit her, she exploded! A boy in the bunker got caught up in the moment; so much so that he threw a grenade, not realizing we'd be caught in the blast. I yelled to stop him, but I was too late. The explosion nearly deafened me, but when the smoke cleared, we were all alive, standing over bloodied Beast bits.

We could not understand what was going on, and crawled out of the bunker. Outside, the few surviving men and women were bathed in the white light, and for the first time we killed Beasts faster than their Queens could spew them. We soon started our counterattack, claiming back first the moon, then clearing out the rest of the galaxy. It was the moment when everything changed, yet no one dares speak of it." He banged an angry fist on the table, raising more dust.

The blonde cleared her throat. "We were shown vids from the Line at the Academy. It was the President's strategy that –"

He cut her off with a tired wave of his hand. "Yeah, yeah, that must have been it. She saved the day. Bah!"

The cadets exchanged awkward looks. "What are you still doing here?" he asked them. "That's the story. There's nothing more to say. Now scram. Leave me alone."

The redhead patted him on the back as the girls moved back to their table, leaving the old man to his thoughts. The blonde made a circling motion with a finger against her temple and winked at the redhead, who nodded and chuckled, stealing a look at the Veteran, hoping he had not caught that. She need not have worried; he had bigger problems than a bunch of doubting cadets. He had seen the hand of God. He knew the world for what it really was.

The bartender standing next to him caught his attention. The young man pointed at the L-shaped medal hanging around the Veteran's neck. "On the house," he said and plonked a half-full bottle on the table, throwing a look of pity at the old man. The old man grunted his thanks as he poured the liquid into his glass. He stared at it, shaking his head and muttering to himself.

###

Mark glanced at the blinking cursor on his monitor, a wicked smile playing on his lips as he punched his keyboard. He paused for a second to check the message his mate had sent him; the one with the cheat code. "Cheat: godMode enable;" appeared on the screen. He hit enter, and the cursor blinked, along with a new message: "Cheat active. God mode enabled."

"Let's see how you like this, you suckers," he mumbled under his breath and unpaused the game.

I Come in Peace

The first time I heard the voice, I was staring into the cup holding my afternoon coffee. At first it was little more than a buzzing in my head, like an orchestra tuning in before the show. I shook my head, wondering if there was something wrong with my ears, when a crystalline voice broke through the noise. "Help me!"

I jumped, startled, spilling coffee on my pyjamas and burning my crotch. Swearing at myself, my eyes darted around the room. I was alone. Of course. Since the accident that cost me both my parents a few years ago, I had avoided people, barely seeing anyone except for the long string of delivery men bringing to my door anything I needed. After their deaths, I had taken a short leave from work to sort things out with the lawyers, organize the funeral and everything. As an only child, all arrangements had fallen on me. Once everything had been completed, the short leave dragged into a long one, then I quit altogether. My parents had left me enough money to support me for life, and I gradually stopped leaving the house. I had no living relatives, and was always too shy to find a girl, so what was there for me to do out there?

The psychologist diagnosed me with depression, but I knew it was just a case of nothing mattering anymore. I had faced the irrevocable truth in life: it ends all too soon, all too suddenly, and nothing we can say or do can change the fact that it's pointless. It may sound bad, but I wasn't unhappy. At least, I don't think I was. The antidepressants might have something to do with that, of course.

Could they be responsible for the voice I just heard? I tried to remember whether we had a history of mental illness in the family. Just what I needed, to be a chainsaw short of a splatter movie. I couldn't remember that much of my extended family. My parents had left behind their brothers and sisters to move to the big city, so I had grown up without any cousins, uncles and aunts. Still, none of them was nuts, as far as I could recall. I listened intently for a moment or two, but heard nothing further. Instead, I caught a whiff of a sweet, flowery smell. I sniffed the air like a hound trying to trace it, but it soon dissipated, so I switched on the telly, convincing myself it had just been my imagination. I went to bed early, still a little shaken by the experience.

When I woke up, the sun was up. In the summer, temperatures in the city rose up well into uncomfortable, and even in the early morning I could tell it would be another scorcher. I headed into the shower, and heard the same noise as last night as soon as I turned on the tap. I stood perfectly still, water pouring on my head, then heard the same voice again: "Don't move!"

Naturally, I did exactly the opposite, and slipped on the wet floor to crash into the bathtub, splashing water all around me. I rubbed my swelling head, groaning, and rose slowly to my feet.

"Please, I need your help," the voice continued.

I was starting to get annoyed, and the pain in my head sent a wave of rage through me. "Who the hell are you?" I yelled.

"I'm sorry, didn't mean to scare you. I've only got a few hours left, and you seem to be the only suitable host I can find."

I stared at myself in the mirror, still clutching my thumping head with one hand. A prematurely aged young man stared back at me, with thick stubble covering his chin and bloodshot eyes. It was the face of someone who had starved himself off experience, his soul demanding nurture. Could this be the reason for my illusions?

I splashed some water on my face, wondering about that last bit. Perhaps I was going crazy, but surely wondering about such a thing meant you're actually sane, right? Or not? I could not tell, and rubbed my face with a towel in an exasperated attempt to make sense of it all.

"Fine," I told the empty room. "What do you want with me?"

"I need your permission to enter."

Awfully good manners for an illusion, I thought as I placed the towel back with a grin on my face. "Sure, whatever," I replied, without giving it a second thought. I mean, if this was an illusion, this voice was already in my head, so what difference could it make?

I gaped in awe as a small orb of light, some ten inches wide, appeared before my eyes. Iridescent rays chased each other within it, like a soap bubble, taking me back to when I was a kid. I watched in awe, mesmerized by the most beautiful sight I had ever seen. The whole thing seemed to rotate, pulsing gently, while various parts inside it rotated at different speeds, creating a kaleidoscope of colours and shapes. *It's so beautiful!*

As I stared at the ball of light, it shot at my chest, bursting into my solar plexus. A sudden numbness spread from my torso to my whole body, as though every cell pulsed and vibrated, resonating to some unheard tune. The sensation slipped from one part of my body to the next, as if the invader tried to make itself comfortable. *If this is a dream, I'll probably wake up at this point.*

I did not. The whole experience lasted but a few seconds, then an immense sense of relief filled me. I guessed it came from the creature when a melodic laughter sounded in my head.

"Thank you," a voice whispered in my head.

"Don't mention it," I said out loud, trying to understand. Then, a moment later, I asked: "What just happened?"

"I needed a host, you accepted me. That's all." I felt a flutter in my chest, as if the creature was happily bouncing around in there.

"That's all?" I asked incredulously of the empty room. "This happens every day, you think?"

"I guess not. You must have some questions." How could a voice in my head sound like it was frowning?

"Some questions! Let's start with what you are, shall we?"

The voice remained silent for a moment, as if trying to frame the answer in as good a way as possible.

"I am mostly what you'd call energy, although that's not exactly right, as I consist of matter, too. It's just, erm... thinner than yours."

Right. That answered it. I tried a different approach. "So, what're you doing here?"

"We've been around for millions of years. You've probably heard of us; your kind calls us ghosts, fairies, will o' the wisps, angels..."

I headed to my laptop and jumped onto the couch. I hit a key and the screen came to life and I punched some keywords into my browser's search field. "Why ain't you with your kind?" I asked, browsing urgently in search of some answers. Millions of results filled the screen, overwhelming me.

"You don't understand. We need hosts, living organisms, to survive. We are not many, but we do share life with you: we are born, we procreate and eventually we, too, will perish. Of course, I'm but a toddler for my kind, although I'm much older than you."

A sudden thought made me pause, startled. "Are you a boy or a girl?"

The voice seemed to giggle. "We don't really have a sex; not like you. But I currently have some characteristics better suited to females."

"Like what?" I asked suspiciously.

The voice seemed to blush, as if that were possible. "I'm pregnant," she said.

I sank into the couch, clutching the laptop. The idea of a pregnant ball of light in me was going to take some getting used to, and I doubted even the all-knowing Internet would offer much help on this.

"So, what did you do before you came to me?"

"My last host died a few days ago. I've been searching for a suitable host since, but couldn't find anyone."

I'm a host. Is that like being possessed, or something? "How do you know who's a suitable host?"

"We feel it, and so do you; a suitable host can sense us. It could be a smell, or a sudden flash at the corner of one's eye. Sometimes you can even hear us."

"The flowers I smelled!" I blurted out.

"Yes, although it's different for everyone. When I realised you could sense me, I tried out different frequencies, as you'd call them, until we communicated. You then had the choice to either help me or not."

"Why does it have to be a person? Couldn't you find an animal?"

"We need a host with developed enough consciousness to survive. An animal can only tolerate us for a limited amount of time before... it becomes too uncomfortable for both of us." My skull tickled me as hair stood on its end at the feelings conveyed by that phrase, almost as if there had been a discharge of static electricity nearby. "We used to be more tolerant," the voice continued, ignoring my rising stress levels, "but we can now only co-exist with you. That's part of the reason why there are so few of us left."

All that took a moment to take in. I made myself a coffee, then threw it away in favour of some chamomile tea. My mom used to make me that to soothe me, and I figured I could use some calming down. I sank back into the couch and continued my mental – in more ways than one – conversation.

"So how did you get here?"

"What, you mean Earth? We can travel everywhere, even on meteorites."

Actually, I meant here, at my home, but it felt good that she could not read my mind.

"Well, give me some time," she protested, much to my dismay. "I just joined you."

"Fine. You were saying?"

"I was explaining that it all started back when you were but chimps climbing trees. Our ancestors were not yet tuned in to your species, so we were able to use them as hosts. We helped the ones we joined survive and multiply. You could say we gave them an evolutionary advantage, and soon they surpassed all other members of their tribes, until they developed a full consciousness."

"The less developed ones must have loved them," I joked.

"More than you realise. They worshipped them, believing them divinely inspired. In a sense, they were, of course. But progress had its cost; after a number of millennia, we couldn't join other species."

"Why would you have to?"

"Because the unexpected happened. After hundreds of thousands of years of symbiosis, people started treating hosts as mentally ill, fearing them. They accused them of devil worshipping, persecuted them, slaughtered them in the thousands. Many of us died then, without an opportunity to join another host."

I remembered my history lessons; man's capacity for cruelty to anyone deemed different, never ceased to amaze me. I had no idea our vicious nature had so much collateral damage.

"Not many do," she agreed.

I should have felt annoyed at her reading my mind, but a new feeling had started filling me. A contentment I had never experienced before; I was one with a creature that accepted my very existence with a deep gratitude. Her appreciation of me seeped into every fibre of my being. I can only compare it to being caught in a snowstorm until you're ready to die of exposure and not even realizing it. Then, someone takes you into a warm room, sits before the stove and hands you a plate of hot soup, until you forget the very notion of cold, the icy death now replaced by cosy contentment. I had never experienced anything like it, and could not imagine living without it. I now understood why people would die to protect this fragile creature that had found its way into my soul.

I can remember little of the following weeks, the days passing like seconds. I was alive again, after two years of numbness. Most of the day I passed chatting with my new friend. She had so much to tell me, so many images to share. I could live every moment she had with her previous hosts, until they felt more real to me than my actual friends. Every story was an immersive experience, consisting of words, images, sounds, flavours... and emotions. Deep emotions, just as real as my own, or even more so. I could *feel* everything these people had felt, caress every lover they had kissed, taste every meal they had enjoyed, listen to every song they had heard. My senses were overflowing with a richness I never imagined possible. Within a few weeks, I had lived entire lifetimes.

Until, one day, it finally hit me. Those people were dead. Their emotions, experiences and lives were little more than memories of my unusual companion. Soon enough, I would be one of them. What could I offer her next host, but a dry, repetitive existence within the four walls of my room? What was a retreat, suddenly felt like a prison, and I longed to walk the streets again, to take advantage of the precious, brief moments of life I had.

I burst the windows open and let the sunlight chase away my drab existence. The sounds of the city hit me with unusual intensity, and I stormed out the door, to re-join life.

Did she make me feel this way? Does she need my experiences, feed on them? She made no comment, but I did not care; it was the right thing to do, I knew, and I wanted to claim back everything I had lost when my parents died. Everything!

I don't remember much of the rest of the day. I visited parks, stared at cars rushing by and fed pigeons and ducks. I walked a lot, ending up at the port, a place I had not visited since I was a child. Hundreds, maybe thousands of people passed me by, ignoring my silent giggles as I gossiped about them with my new friend.

The setting sun found me sitting on a bench, facing the water. It was the most beautiful sunset I could remember, bringing tears of joy to my eyes. When the last thin sliver of the golden disk sank into the ocean, I rubbed my eyes and started to get up. This was the best day I'd had in years, I decided.

A sudden shiver ran up and down my spine, and my guts clenched involuntarily. "What's wrong?" I asked, as a feeling of dread filled my heart.

"We should go," the Voice implored in my head. For the first time since we had joined, she sounded apprehensive; scared even.

"Why do –" I started to complain, but decided against it. Her fear was too real for me to ignore it, even though it made no sense to me. Anyway, watching the thinning crowds, I realized I was getting tired.

I walked faster and faster, until her urgency made me run down the street. I took a backstreet shortcut towards the metro station; it would be the fastest way back. As soon as I started down the poorly-lit alley, I realized it was a bad idea. This was the sort of place where bad things happened, I decided, and spun around to head back to the main street. A punch to my stomach took me by surprise, and I found myself on all fours on the dusty ground, trying to catch my breath.

Truth be told, I did not even feel the pain; the shock was too great for that. It's just that one moment I was standing, then the next I was crawling on the dusty backstreet, trying to figure out what had happened. I started to get up, when every muscle in my body contracted and expanded in rapid succession, making me scream in pain. Out of the corner of my eye, I caught a silhouette with a silver cylinder, like a small rod. Blue sparks, like tiny lightning, burst from its tip to enter my chest at the same point where the Voice had entered.

Through half-open eyes I saw the sparks rip out a ball of light from my body. It twisted and turned in a grotesque way as it exited my flesh, its colours now changed. It seemed to suffer; I could feel her pain adding to mine as it tore away to enter the cylinder, netted by the lightning.

When the cylinder sucked her inside, it snapped shut with a hiss. The sparks finally died, leaving me fighting for breath. I moaned and tried to crawl up, every cell in my body aching. It was more than physical pain; I felt empty, as if part of my very soul had been ripped out.

The shadow behind the cylinder leaned forward, coming into sharp focus. A man caught me by the shoulders, not ungently, and helped me to my feet. With my back against the wall, I ended up sitting on the pavement. He patted me down, as if searching for injuries, and I had a chance to examine him. His tired, prematurely aged face was lit up by too kind eyes. A long, dark coat, completely inappropriate for the warm season, covered him from head to toe. God knows what else was hidden in its pockets, beside the cylinder.

"You're gonna be fine," he murmured as soon as he finished his cursory exam. His self-assured voice betrayed efficiency.

"Who are you?" I mumbled. My tongue felt swollen in my mouth, making it hard to speak.

"Not important. What's important is that we got to you in time."

"For what?" I asked, hoping he did not hear the bitterness in my voice.

"You had a parasite. Not only that, it was pregnant. Had I not removed it, you might have a few months left, maybe even weeks."

My eyes opened wide. "You're lying!" I blurted out. He gave me a questioning look, and I hastened to explain. "I spoke to her." I cringed, as I bit my tongue. Ignoring the pain, I continued. "She's my friend!"

The man chuckled. "Yeah, it can look that way. Since you spoke to it, it must have told you where they're from. Did it also tell you its species is no longer compatible with ours?"

I shook my head, too weak to protest. "She said we grew up together. I mean, her species and ours did."

"Sure. But we haven't been compatible in ages. No longer than a few months, anyway; a couple of years at the most. That's why people turned against them. When pregnant, they're really dangerous – and I'll be damned if I know how they get pregnant in the first place."

I avoided his eyes. "How dangerous?"

"Some ninety percent of the cases lead to death or coma when they give birth. I guess our nervous system is overloaded. Maybe it didn't use to be like that, maybe we were hardier as a species. Who knows. All I know is, you're one lucky kid; a few weeks, and she'd have given birth."

He raised himself to his feet and studied the cylinder, clicking small indentations on its otherwise smooth surface.

I stared at him for a while, gathering my thoughts. "How did you find me?"

"I followed its pheromones. When it enters a new host, it releases special chemicals –"

"I know what pheromones are," I interrupted him.

"Well, we had traced the parasite to its last host, but it gave us the slip. Our sniffers caught it." He glanced at my questioning face and cleared his throat. "They're special stations looking out for pheromones. All big cities have a couple of sniffers. Anyway, we picked it up at the port. I was sent to capture it."

"So what happens now?"

"We never met, and you go home."

"Not me, her."

He glanced at the cylinder and shrugged. "The parasite? I only collect them; others will dispose of it."

He might have saved me, but the emptiness inside me hurt like an open wound. The man spun around and started down the street, still fiddling with the cylinder. I pushed down to get up, and my hand touched something metallic. I felt the round shape of a lead pipe under my fingers, and clutched it. Before I knew what I was doing, I was on my feet, lunging at the man, pipe in the air. It crashed against his head, sending him to the ground.

"Oh no, no, no," I mumbled in panic as I saw blood gushing from a cut on his head. The pipe slipped through trembling fingers to crash on the ground.

The man lay still, and I touched his throat, trying to stop my hand from shaking. I sighed in relief when I felt his pulse beat under my fingers, and grabbed the cylinder. I took off as fast as my legs would take me, trying to pry it open. The damned thing would not budge. Still running, I beat the cylinder against the wall beside me. It took three hits before the lid flew off. A ball of shimmering light darted out and flew away.

"Where are you going?" I shouted. "Come on!"

It hovered in the middle of the street for a moment, undecided. "What are you waiting for? Come!" I repeated.

It dashed towards me and burst into my chest, filling me with terror mixed with relief. The emotions threatened to swallow me, but I somehow managed to reach my home and rushed inside, to safety.

I sank into the couch with a loud sigh. She had not said a word since entering me, but her presence filled me, comforted me. I could tell she was calmer now, and my own heartbeat finally started slowing down.

"Why?"

Her question startled me. I did not answer for a while, shuddering at the memory of my life without her, and the dreaded loneliness she had put an end to.

"Why did you save me?" she insisted. "Aren't you afraid I'll kill you?"

"There are worse things than death," I murmured in the end. "Besides, we still have a ten percent chance of making it, right? Grow old together... Maybe on an island somewhere, where we'll be safe."

I let out a loud groan as I raised myself to my feet to switch off the light, before crawling to bed.

A Fresh Start

"Move! Step aside for our master!"

The voice of my guards riding before my comfortable carriage startled me from my nap. I must have dozed off, missing the last part of the journey. Stifling a yawn, I pulled slightly aside the thick curtains to look outside the window. Behind the backs of the people bowing respectfully before us, I could see my mansion, sitting atop the lush hill overlooking the city. It looked splendid, with the setting sun painting it gold and the twin moons rising behind it. It was part of the vast complex of buildings that formed the Emperor's palace. Then again, everything in this world was part of the Emperor's property. Since he usually did as I instructed him, I guess that made the whole world mine. Not bad for a simple builder!

And to think it had all started as a simple prank.

Fifteen years had already passed since that day. My past life seemed so far away – and yet, like only yesterday. I drew the curtain back to sink heavily onto my silk pillows. My mind was drawn back to that day, when I was still working as a simple builder in Athens. I had been an engineer in my own country, but after the war I gave all my money to the dubious characters who had promised me a new beginning. What else was there to do? Had I stayed back home, I may have ended up dead – or worse, been recruited by one of the many militias that sprung up daily.

The trip to Europe had been harder than expected, but in the end I managed to arrive at Europe's south-eastern corner. After years of living in a semi-legal status, I managed to scrape together enough to get a work permit. Mercifully, I did not have much to spend my money on. I had no family back home, having lost my wife in the war, and I never did like drinking. Nothing to do with my religion; it just upset my stomach. It was the same with women; I avoided the kind of women who could suck you dry before leaving you for their next victim; not because of my ethics, but because the memory of my wife was still too fresh and painful. So, I found myself an immigrant in a land with a schizoid attitude towards us. In the many buildings I worked on, I met some people from my country and we joined our loneliness.

My best friend had probably been Arak. A heart of gold, but so gullible and superstitious. Naturally, this made him a perfect target for our teasing. One night we were eating kebabs, gossiping about our boss' latest girlfriend, a plastic brunette with blond roots, when Arak stared at us and announced that he had something important to say. Stealing careful glances around, he whispered that he had found out about a haunted building right next to where we worked. It used to belong to a rich family, he said, but no-one would step in nowadays, for many people had disappeared there. I almost choked on my kebab, but it seemed that he was serious. He gave me a stern look and started to count the people who had supposedly disappeared after entering the house. We all laughed at him and teased him all night, until he angrily dared us to go there and see for ourselves. Since we had all had some ouzo – even me – we accepted immediately.

Our reaction startled poor Arak; he must have thought we would have rejected his daredevil suggestion. He started to mumble that he didn't mean it, but of course that only made us more daring and we practically carried him there, forcing him to show us the way.

The notorious house was an impressive mansion that had obviously seen better days. It must have been built in the 19th century, when rich merchants hired famous architects like Kleanthis, Schaubert, Hansen and Ziller to display their wealth. Typically eclectic, it combined many different styles of its time. I stared at it admiringly, ignoring the many wounds time had inflicted on it. Like most of these houses, with the happy exception of a lucky few that were rescued by a shipping company or a bank, it had been left to rot. I felt sorry for it, but there was not much I could do, so I pushed the heavy door that smelled of rotten wood and decay. It gave a deep sigh as it opened, sending Arak to fly away in a frenzied gallop. He paused only for a moment at the gate to plead with us not to enter, but this only served to make us laugh even harder before swaggering inside.

The house was all dark, but many windows were broken and a sickly yellow light from the street squeezed through. It was the kind of place that would normally serve as a squatters' hideout; I was somewhat surprised to find it empty. What was particularly eerie were the silhouettes of some old, forgotten furniture, covered in thick dust; I was sure the house would have been cleaned up by now. Perhaps the building's notoriety served a purpose after all. As it were, even the oil paintings on the walls were intact, creating an eerie, haunting atmosphere, as if we were walking amidst the remnants of a long-gone past.

I stood before one of the paintings, studying a stern-looking lady, grim enough to grant plausibility to Arak's fears. It seemed her gaze made me forget myself, as I realized I had been left alone in the room when an invisible breath of cold wind shut the big door behind me with a loud bang. Although I had a healthy disrespect of anything fantastic, I hate to admit I was getting spooked. The fact that the rest of the gang seemed to have disappeared somewhere deep in the house's bowels did not help either. I went to the door and tried to pry it open, but it was stuck. It was no wonder in such an old house; the wood must have expanded and contracted with the weather countless times in its century of life. Still, I found myself wondering what to do next.

I absent-mindedly took out a fag from my pocket and reached for my lighter. For some reason, I found it hard to light it and had to turn towards the wall, to protect the fragile flame from any sudden gusts. When I finally managed to light the cigarette, I drew the smoke in with a deep, guilty pleasure and exhaled towards the crumbling plaster. I gazed at it, realizing with a start what was wrong with it. The smoke seemed to be drawn into a narrow crack on the wall. I placed my hand on it, noticing a fine draft.

I started patting the wall lightly, looking for an opening, and pushing various bumps on it. One of them gave way and the wall sprung open abruptly, revealing a doorway. I glanced nervously behind me before crossing into the darkness. As soon as I had done so, the wall closed behind me, just as abruptly as it had opened. For a moment I panicked and started scratching it, trying in vain to push it open. Failing to do so, I noticed a flickering sliver of light, and spun around to make my way towards it. It seemed to emanate from the thin opening between another door and the floor. Upon reaching it, I pushed, nearly soiling myself at the sight of a lush, sunlit field.

When someone has such an experience, it can be hard for the mind to comprehend it. In its effort to explain what's happening, it starts coming up with alternative explanations: *perhaps I've died and am in Heaven.* Or *maybe this is but a dream.* It's like a car switching gears awkwardly; it jerks momentarily, trying to regain its balance. That's the reason why it took me so long to notice the pretty young girl staring patiently at me, fiddling with a shiny metal object. Her long, green dress highlighted her emerald eyes. *Heaven. This must be Heaven,* I thought when I finally did notice her. I opened my mouth to say something, but nothing came out. So, I was left gazing, mouth open. Mercifully, she was more experienced at this than me. She approached me gently, cleared her throat, glanced once more at the gadget in her hands as to confirm something, and simply said, "Hello".

My mind gave up trying to figure this one out, so the only response I could give was just as surreal. "Hi. How are you?"

"Fine, just fine," came the chirpy reply. I was lost for words, when I realized: the conversation was not in English, but in my native language.

"You speak…" She nodded towards a pin on her chest, anticipating my question.

"It's my instant translator. We can communicate in any language you wish."

Since this was not the most improbable thing so far, I simply nodded and waited for her to continue. "You must be wondering where you are. If you're up for it, I can answer some questions. Unless you'd rather rest a bit. Some have more trouble with the transition than others."

My curiosity was greater than any tiredness, so I finally managed to close my still-open mouth, nodding emphatically. I studied her smooth skin and long, flowing hair cascading over her bare shoulders. This was a woman I could easily fall in love with.

"Good," she continued, throwing me an appreciative glance. "Just how familiar are you with the universe's structure?"

I felt someone was pulling my leg, but had no idea who or why. "I know it's big," was the first thing I could think of.

She gave me a disapproving look before lecturing me in a teacher-like manner. "The universe you know is just one of many. Think of the foam in the bathtub. Each bubble is one universe. You live on the surface of one of these bubbles, but, given the right circumstances, could hop to a different one – an adjacent universe. Is that clear?"

To this day, I wonder what one might answer to that. "Sure," was the only thing I could think of.

She now threw me a satisfied look. "Good. The place where you were standing a moment ago was a gate, a portal if you like, between universes. You shouldn't have found it actually; I thought we had hidden it rather well."

She seemed puzzled, so I offered to clarify things for her. "It was the smoke," I explained.

Her smooth brow creased, then she shook her head. "It doesn't really matter. What's important is that you're here now."

"Where *is* here?" I asked, trying to sound as nonchalant as possible.

"You are in a world that no longer exists," she said sadly. "Our world was the first to bridge the gap between the various universes. Unfortunately, the temptation of immigration turned out to be too great for us to resist."

"Immigration?"

"Of course," she replied emphatically, as if that somehow clarified matters. "Imagine you can travel anywhere in the worlds: worlds now starting off and worlds at the apex of their glory and power. You may be a mediocre musician in your world, when in another world you could be the most renowned composer in history. One moment you are a simple nurse, the next you're mankind's best-known doctor and adored saviour. What would you do?" She raised her shoulders without waiting for a reply.

"Are you saying that everyone has left your world?"

"A few of us stayed behind on principle. Others have returned to die at home. And some realized that no matter how far you run, you can't escape your problems; you take them with you." A soft sigh escaped her lips, and we both remained silent for a moment, while I was trying to figure all this out.

"So, anyone I know from your world?" it occurred to me to ask.

"Probably. You ever heard of Bach?"

"Johann Sebastian Bach?" I cried out, my eyes opening wide. "He was one of you?"

"Of course. How do you think one man could compose so much music in a single lifetime? He pillaged all our music and ran away to your world. It was the same with Bill."

"Bill?"

"I think he chose the name Shakesleaf when he left for your world," she said, pursing her lips in her effort to remember. Part of me wanted to taste those cute lips, but the name made me open my eyes wide.

"Shakespeare?"

"That's it!" Her face beamed. "He was a classmate, you know. Nice kid. Could have been a great author, but preferred to steal our plays and off he went. So many followed them... They pillaged our world and left. Nothing original is ever created here anymore – we are no more than a shadow of our former selves."

I felt sorry for her, but an idea started forming in my head. "You mean I, too, can go anywhere I choose?"

She glanced at me with forlorn eyes. "Sure. What have you studied?"

"I used to be an engineer, but am working as a builder at the moment."

"We could use someone like you: young, gifted, not afraid of work... and cute," she added after a second's hesitation. "How would you like to stay here?" she asked, her voice betraying hidden hope.

I won't say I wasn't tempted, but the possibilities far exceeded staying in a broken world, no matter how charming the company. "Perhaps. But I could go anywhere I wanted to, right?"

She hung her head. "Yes. Our culture respects nothing more than free will. That's why we haven't tried to stop anyone from fleeing. If you want, I can take you anywhere you wish."

I felt a little sorry for her, but at the same time my heart thumped in my chest. A fire, one whose very existence I had ignored for all these years, burned deep within me. Ambition rushed through my veins, driven by the opportunity to be anyone I wanted, by the exciting possibilities in front of me. "I want everything! I want to be respected and feared by everyone!" The words that flew from my mouth surprised me, but it was the truth. I had a burning ambition, I realized for the first time in my life, and no-one would stand in its way. After years of having people look down on me, of fearing what tomorrow would bring, I wanted nothing more than the desire to fear and want for nothing any more. Never again!

Her eyes betrayed a surprising understanding as she simply said, "As you wish."

I spent the following days studying the multiverse. There were so many worlds – too many to count. Some were so advanced it made one dizzy even to look at them; but what would I want there? I would only be notable as a monument of stupidity compared to everyone. Others were too primitive for my taste. No matter how driven I was, my desires were tempered by a healthy wish to live in comfort – and not lose my head by a giant, ape-like barbarian. I needed to pick a place not too far off culturally from the one I had left. A world that would allow me to rise rapidly thanks to my skills and knowledge, but also one where I would not face prejudice because of my colour, age, gender or whatever. In the end I picked the perfect candidate, and spent many months with my new friend studying its culture.

We came close during those months, but I never allowed myself to admit just how close. After all, I had made up my mind. I was leaving her. Part of me wanted to stay, but it was the fiery part, the one awakened by the unanticipated opportunity, that guided my actions.

As a parting gift, she gave me a translator to help me. To her credit, she never once tried to convince me to stay. She saw my relentless ambition, a sight she must have witnessed only too often in the past, and probably knew she would just be wasting her breath. When I was about to leave, she handed me another thing as well, similar to the gadget she was holding the first time we had met.

"It's a Tracker," she explained.

"A what?"

"A device that can find the contact point between two universes. Should you wish to return to my world someday..." Her voice trailed off for a moment. "Or to any world, for that matter." She avoided my gaze as she pointed to round dials on its smooth surface to explain how the device worked.

"Maybe I'll pop back for a visit," I said with a forced grin.

A sad smile played on her lips. "Having already travelled twice within the multiverse, I would advise you against it. It would be best if you thought of this as a one-way ticket."

"So I'm stuck there? What if –"

She raised a hand to stop me, her face now deadly serious. "Travelling this way is exponentially dangerous. Everything should be fine this time, but if you decide to travel anywhere else, that will have to be your final trip. That's why most people never came back."

She spun around without looking at me, to walk me to a plain wooden door, standing eerily in the middle of the field where we had first met. I was sad to leave her, but at the same time my heart fluttered with excitement, my eyes already fixed on the door. We parted with a simple goodbye and I pushed the handle to step inside.

After a short walk down a dark corridor, I opened a second door to find myself surrounded by a dense forest. I spotted a narrow trail leading to a small village, then turned my head upwards. The sun was playing through thick leaves with unfamiliar shapes. Exotic smells attacked my nostrils, and I took in the flowery fragrances with a deep breath. After sneezing a couple of times, I made my way to meet my first people in this new world, a wide grin plastered on my face.

My friend had taught me well, and even given me enough currency to live out my life in comfort, if I so wished. This was not enough, though. Upon talking with the natives, I confirmed that I had chosen my new home well. My basic scientific and technical knowledge was advanced enough to impress everyone.

A few months later, I left that village and my new friends behind, to move to the capital. My fame had been growing rapidly, and the Emperor himself had asked to see me. It was easy enough to impress him, since I knew more than everyone else in his court combined. So, he asked me to teach his son and heir. After that, things were easy. I used my position to become irreplaceable at the palace, while staying away from any intrigue or politics. I encouraged the Emperor to build aqueducts and irrigation channels. Thanks to better water management, agricultural production grew exponentially and I convinced the Emperor to build granaries for the extra production. When a couple of years later there was a drought, people were grateful for his foresight. At the same time, proper hygiene, waste management and drainage works ensured a dramatic drop in mortality rates. Basic stuff, but put together they meant that the people had never lived longer, nor better. The Emperor was worshipped like a god, and I was his right-hand man.

Naturally, not everyone was happy by all this. Every paradise has its serpent, and this one had the barons. The ever-scheming lords who wished to become Emperors hated me for strengthening his position. Little under a year ago, some generals even tried a coup – surely at some baron's urging, although this was never proven. In the end, the conspiracy was exposed and the Emperor went after them, showing little mercy. I was not happy with the harsh way he treated them, but was unable to convince him to show leniency. For a time, I was afraid this might lead to reprisals or an uprising, but I was proven mistaken. For now at least, the situation seemed more stable than ever. The people loved him and I had everything I had ever wished for in my life.

I chuckled as I thought of the huge, sparkling diamonds under my seat. They were given to me for the Emperor; a gift to sign the peace treaty between ours and a neighbouring country. A peace treaty I had orchestrated, I might add. Their king needed the extra food stored in our granaries and we needed the spoils from his merchant activities. His kingdom was renowned for its gems, as the small box between my legs could attest.

I placed a foot on it, its surface hard and cold under my sole. Leaning back, I let out a deep sigh. These diamonds were but stones after all, just like gold was but a particularly cold and heavy metal. What I longed for was real friendship; not the constant stream of lackeys, spies and bootlickers that swarmed the palace.

I could have any woman I wanted, and more riches and power than I had ever dreamed of. But I knew everyone schemed behind my back, and my nights were restless, interrupted by memories of my time with the emerald-eyed woman I had long left behind. A simpler, quieter time. My hair had thinned and greyed out, and the daily responsibilities of running a country weighed heavily on my shoulders. I could not resign, of course; disobeying the Emperor this way would amount to treason. Nor could I take a vacation. I had tried it only once, only to spend months afterwards, trying to undo the damage to the state inflicted by my replacements.

Thoughts of the sweet young girl on a forlorn planet filled my head with increasing frequency. She had warned me against attempting the travel again, but had the time come to ignore her warning? Was I ready to give all this up? And if I did, where would I go; back to Earth or back to her?

A sudden jerk and scared shouts interrupted my thoughts. I glanced nervously outside. It was getting dark now, but in the dwindling light I saw people running away. Guards on horses passed me by, galloping towards some unseen enemy.

The wagon came to an abrupt halt and I heard a loud crash outside. The carriage crushed forward, sending me to fly and bump my head against the velvet-covered wall. The door flew open and my driver burst in, a large axe in his hands. It was a formidable weapon, with a long spike in the back and a sharp steel semicircle at the front. Still dazed from the shock, I yelped in alarm at the sight of murder in his eyes; a sight I remembered well from my home country, a lifetime away. He lunged at me and instinct kicked in, making me jump to the side. His axe dug itself into the panelled wood inches from me, and I took the opportunity to kick him in the gut while he tried to free it. He groaned and took a step back, then reached for the axe again. A second kick sent him crashing against the floor and gave me the time to dash out of the door.

Arrows flew around me, and I let out a surprised cry as a flaming arrow scratched my shoulder to impale itself quivering on the wood before me. Its flames licked the carriage, sending acrid smoke to rise and bringing tears to my eyes. My mind was spinning as I put the fire out with my coat, but more arrows followed, sending flames to engulf the carriage.

I threw the smoking coat out and jumped back inside and prepared to repel a renewed attack. My driver now had a dagger in his hands as he charged me, having given up on his axe, still stuck in the wall. I managed to get out of the way of his blade and ducked behind him, spinning around to face him again. He now had his back to the door and our eyes locked.

"Why?" I asked him, trying to catch my breath.

His shoulders rose. "The Barons pay well," he growled and charged me for a third time. I leaned sideways and pushed him with my left hand, as my right one pulled his coat. He lost his balance and crashed on the wall behind me.

Once again I swung around, expecting another attack. The sickening smell of death filled the small space and the man made a strange gurgling noise, his back still turned to me, his hands raised before his throat in silent pleading. I took an apprehensive step towards him and kicked his leg once, then twice, before noticing the end of the axe's spike protruding from his neck. His limbs flailed for a moment, then he was still.

Sick rose to my mouth and I rushed out again, without thinking. More whistling arrows greeted me, impaling themselves into the carriage, quivering all around me, sending me to duck back inside the wagon. I had ignored the driver's last words in my panic, but it belatedly dawned on me that the Barons must have ambushed us solely to get rid of me. They probably thought that, if they can't get the Emperor, they might as well get the man behind his success.

This complicated matters. My guards might be prepared to repel a bandit attack, but an attack orchestrated by the battle-hardened barons was a different thing altogether; they must have put much thought in preparing this. I might have been avoiding politics all along, but politics had found me in the end. Wild shouts and cries rang all around me, and I had no doubt the conspirators would be defeated. By the time they had, though, I would be burned to a crisp. The horses had been freed by the traitorous driver, and I had nowhere to go.

I clutched my head and breathed deeply, trying not to panic. This only served to send me coughing, as the smoke around me thickened. I swore and made one last, desperate attempt to get out, but a thick swarm of arrows flew my way. One of them scratched my eyebrow, and I had no option but to withdraw back to the relative safety of the carriage as a trail of blood threatened to blind me. I grabbed a silk pillow to fight thick flames; I could not stay there much longer. The air was hardly breathable by now, and I would probably be unconscious or worse by the time the palace lancers joined my guards. The thought of what they would do to our attackers was of small consolation. The real question was how to get away alive.

Kneeling on the floor where the smoke was thinner, I pulled out the chain around my neck, revealing the Tracker. I always carried it with me; not because I thought I might need it, but for sentimental reasons. I always considered myself a romantic deep inside, and holding it within my hand gave me a sense of nostalgia for the life I had left behind, together with pride for my achievements since. And yet, my silly sentimentalism might yet save my life. I could hardly see its silver surface through the choking smoke and the blood trickling down my eyes. I was about to hit the controls that would send me safely back, when a thought occurred to me. With sweaty fingers, I pried the box open and grabbed as many gems as I could fit in my deep pockets while trying to steady my hand from shaking.

The inside of the carriage was hotter than a furnace, but my thumb hovered above the button that would send me home. Where would I head? I had enough gems to last me a lifetime on Earth. Power, money, fame; anything I ever longed for. Everything I had lost because of the scheming Barons would be mine again. I turned the dial to Earth, as the girl had shown me.

Her memory made my hand freeze. I had already chosen one world over her once. Was I really going to make the same choice a second time? I coughed violently to expel acrid smoke from my lungs as her last words rang in my head: "If you decide to travel anywhere else, that will have to be your final trip." It's strange how I had not thought of that once all these years, but her words now weighed down on me like an unbearable burden. *Be reasonable,* a voice whispered in my head. *Will she even be available after all these years? How sure are you of her feelings, anyway? What if you've misread her?* The Tracker almost slipped through my sweaty, trembling fingers. I had the hardest choice in my life to make, and just a precious few seconds to do so.

My pocket burst into flames, and I put it out with my hand in panic, sending sparkling gems to rain onto the floor. A wide smile crept on my lips as I ignored them to click the dial. It made no difference if I arrived empty-handed; I had no use for gems where I was going. It was time for a fresh start.

The Sentry

The sentry froze in place to sniff the brisk night air. He caught a hint of the familiar scent of decomposition and death that accompanied the Monster's arrival, although he could neither see nor hear it yet. He always prided himself on his keen sense of smell, knowing it had served him well in the past. The scent could only mean one thing; that the beast would arrive any minute now. He paced along his patrol route in eager anticipation. Tonight was the night; tonight, he would exact his revenge.

Every night during these past months, ever since they posted him to his new station, he had been terrified of the Monster. He had followed his Family there, the one they had assigned him to protect, unaware of the threat that came with his new post. His mind drifted to the first time he had laid eyes on it... With a shudder, he tried to shake away the awful memory. This was not the time to think of that, he reflected. His thoughts should be on how proud his Family would be, when he showed them his trophy, the Monster's head on a stick. Or something similar; he had not really considered the details. There would be plenty of time for that, once the hideous thing was finally dealt with. In his mind he could already see their beaming faces as they congratulated him on his bravery; an image that filled him with bliss. His achievement would please them for sure; how could it not? They had to hate the Sacrifice at least as much as he did.

Day after day, the Monster chugged along at the crack of dawn to steal away all the precious food they had gathered during their long, arduous day. He hated to watch them slave away under the blistering sun, only to put away the juiciest, most prized morsels within the ritual urn. Despite the Sacrifice, they were well fed of course, but that did not stop him from resenting the fact that they had to make do with the scraps, while the Monster gobbled up the most aromatic, delicious parts of their provisions. Perhaps others had resigned themselves to the situation, but not him: he had no qualms dealing with the Monster once and for all.

His face lit up as a sudden thought occurred to him. Maybe this was the very reason they had handed him this assignment. There were many others who could patrol the area, but they had chosen *him* for the job. Could it be that, deep inside, they *wanted* him to put an end to the Sacrifice; to conduct the forbidden rebellion on their behalf? To stand up against their oppressor, the thief of their food and their future?

His chest swelled with pride. *I won't let them down*, he promised himself. He would end the Sacrifice, and then they would, at last, enjoy all the food they spent every waking hour collecting. And who knows; perhaps that might even mean more food for him.

His mouth watered at the mental image of the exquisite titbits now ending up in the ritual urn; the tastiest bits offered to the

Monster. They would be so proud at his achievement, they might even share some of these with him. His stomach growled, and he remembered he had not eaten since morning. *Should I head back for a snack? It seems to be running late tonight, anyway. Perhaps it won't come tonight.* He stopped his pacing to shift his weight first on one leg, then another, filled with trepidation mixed with hidden relief.

Before reaching a decision, a low rumble caught his attention. The hair on his neck shot up, making him resemble a tiny dinosaur, and a brief wave of panic washed over his chest. He cursed himself for allowing his reverie to distract him long enough for the Monster to approach. The cool air carried its horrible moan as it staggered along the narrow streets. Then, he made out its silhouette in the thin light of dawn. It was close; closer than he had realized! He ducked under some bushes to wait, his heart pounding in his ears.

Within seconds, the Monster reached the end of the sentry's patrol area. A street lamp lit it from behind, sending its long shadow to the spot where he lay hidden. He watched it stagger towards the neighbours' ritual urn. Although too far to see clearly, the sentry knew by heart the scene that would now play out. The beast's uniformed lackeys would emerge to examine the urn's contents. *What'd happen if the offering was deemed unsatisfactory?* he wondered. He had no idea, but knew that the neighbours would never dare offend the Monster that way.

Stealing a peek in its direction, he saw the beast lurching nearby, its hideous nose sniffing the ground. The lackeys waited patiently for it to growl its consent and stop, quivering in eager anticipation. They approached the urn in slow, authoritative steps. Lifting it onto the air, they exchanged some words; most likely a prayer, or invocation of some sort. Then, they emptied its contents with one swift motion straight into the beast's ravenous mouth. The Monster ground and gulped down the delicious offering, moaning in sickening satisfaction as it enjoyed the mouth-watering, aromatic provisions. It lay down, a gentle quiver running through its deformed body, while crunching the Sacrifice, waiting for the lackeys to jump back on its back.

He knew the sequence well, for he had been watching the Monster's every movement in silent, wary observation ever since he took the post. It had become his nightmare, and many a morning he would wake up in speechless terror after dreaming of its repulsive mouth closing around him, crunching his flesh and bones into tiny, mangled bits. *No more nightmares*, he promised himself. *Tonight, it ends.*

He dug deeper into the bushes. The Monster scared him more than anything in the entire world, and his whole body trembled with anticipation, overloaded glands pumping adrenaline into his frail body. Courage might be his only weapon, but he did not care: his faith would prevail.

He ran his plan once again through his head. It was really very simple; the Monster's slow stagger suggested poor eyesight, despite its bug eyes. Also, it had trouble turning its revolting head, and always stumbled as it made its way backwards. All the sentry had to do, then, was to attack from behind, while the lackeys examined the ritual urn, leaving their master unguarded. Thick, impenetrable scales covered its body, so he would target its soft legs, in the hope of wounding it enough to immobilize it, thus preventing it from fleeing. Then, he would fight its assistants, taking them out one at a time. With any luck, they would only notice him when it was too late.

While he gathered his courage, the Monster let a satisfied sigh and the two men returned the neighbour's urn to its place. The beast moaned and rose on its legs, causing the ground to shudder under its vile, painfully slow crawl towards his family's urn. A moment later, its sparkling gaze fell on the bush. It never ceased to amaze him how bright the creature's eyes were, and he lowered his head in nervous apprehension.

He sealed his eyes until the Monster was so close that he could smell its awful breath, then opened them again to stare at it through the bushes' thick leaves. Things were going to plan so far; the Monster had not noticed him. It staggered and stopped before him, sniffing loudly at the ground. The lackeys jumped off, exchanged a few words and approached the urn.

The sentry gulped and steeled himself. A silent prayer in his mind, he let out a loud cry and charged at the beast. He grabbed one of its thick legs, but in vain; the Monster did not even seem to register his presence. In desperation, he bit its leathery hide as hard as he could and clawed at it, in a futile effort to tear off a tendon. The skin was too hard for him, though, and the beast proved impervious to pain. No matter how hard he tried, his teeth failed to break the skin.

Approaching footsteps startled him, making him realize he had forgotten the lackeys in his frenzied state. They closed in on him, had him cornered now, a cruel smirk on their lips. His body trembled in fear; he had wasted precious time, and took a frightened step back as they crept menacingly towards him.

With a clarity of mind that surprised even him, he measured the distance separating him from the safety of the bushes behind them; his family's bushes. They would never dare to enter there, would they? It would be unheard of. *So would attacking the Monster*, a voice whispered in his mind. He shook his head to make it stop; this was not the time to second-guess himself.

He took a deep breath before dashing towards the two men. One of them stumbled in his effort to grab him, crashing to the ground. The sentry jumped over him, a strong jerk of his legs leading him to fly straight into the bush. Crawling as fast as he could through leaves dripping with morning dew, he emerged behind it and knelt down, trying to become one with the aromatic, moist soil. He lay there, observing the lackeys' attempts to figure out where he'd gone, his heart beating faster than ever as he tried to catch his breath. A silent grin of satisfaction appeared on his face as it became clear that he had escaped them. He pushed his head onto the ground as a beam of light flickered over the bush, pleased that they did not dare enter his family's space.

One of them leaned down to examine their master's wounded leg. *I may have wounded it so badly they'll think twice before stealing our food again*, he thought with pride. He may not have been able to defeat it, but he had taught it a lesson it would not forget any time soon.

The two men exchanged a few words before heading towards the bush. For a moment it looked as if they'd do the unthinkable and enter his family's space. *I told you; it's no more unthinkable than what* you *did¸* the voice in his head scolded him. His heart skipped a beat and every muscle in his body tightened, as he steeled himself for battle. The men hesitated for a moment, then spun around to jump back on the beast. A loud sigh escaped his lips and his eyes lit up. *That's right, run, you cowards*, he thought, watching the Monster continue its insatiable walk through the narrow streets.

###

As the garbage truck chugged along, a puzzled driver glanced back towards the garden into which the puppy had disappeared. "What's wrong with that dog?" he yelled at his mate, loud enough to be heard over the engine's clatter. "Why did he attack our tires?" Instead of an answer, his colleague raised his shoulders, his eyes already fixed on the next trashcan.

Big Bang

By Amos M. Carpenter

His little sister had grasped the basics of the game much faster than he had believed possible. With a few brilliant moves, miniscule changes in the initial placements of less than eighty billion atoms, she had left the delicate balance of Creation intact, but had extended the timeline by an extra sixteen thousand years.

Now, however, it was time to show her how a true master played the game. What exactly had she done, anyway? Al studied the difference between the two game stages fastidiously for a moment, then he saw it. A slow grin spread over his face.

"Very clever," he said after altering the comm settings to Private Message so that the comment would only reach his sister in her room next door. He had installed the game on her set only last night. *Unreal*, he thought to himself, *she must've been up all night to learn the controls that quickly.* "Ready for the real thing?"

"Yep," her voice squealed inside his ears, "if they'll let me play."

"Lemme handle that." He changed the settings back to Game Broadcast. "I'm back, guys, didjas miss me? Only got half an hour before lunch though, just got an external PM from my mum. Hey, my sis wants to join up today, 'kay? Her name's Go."

"Long as she doesn't wipe us all out in her first move," Bud snickered.

"Not *all* of you," Go replied. "Not in the first move, anyway."

It earned her one of Zeke's snorting laughs. Mark giggled in the background.

"She replacing you, Al?" Kathy was her usual humourless self, brisk and businesslike. "Or as a brand new player?"

"New player. Objections? No? Good. Adding you to the game, Go. What name?"

"Convention is to start with the first few letters of our real names," Zeke explained. "Like, Kathy is 'Kali', I'm 'Zeus'. So you're Go... something."

"Okay," Go said. "I'll be 'God', then."

"What, just 'God'?" Bud sounded incredulous.

"Uh, yep."

"If that's what she wants... 'God' added to the game. Since you're new, sis, we'll let you have the first turn."

"Aw, come on," Mark protested.

"She's the Game Master's little sister, Mark, what did you expect?" Kathy's tone was dripping with cynicism.

"Guys," Al sighed, "stop whining, will ya? If you *really* think it's so unfair, vote someone else to be GM for the next game. What's she gonna do, huh? 'Sides, how else is she gonna get into the game with half a chance, can anyone tell me that? Didn't *think* so." Al switched to PM Go with a grin. "Told you I'd handle it. Now show 'em what you've got. Just like the practice scenario, only a little more complex." Back to GB again. "Okies then. Everyone ready?"

Four ready signals lit up simultaneously at the top right of Al's internal vision. A fifth, Go's, lit up two seconds later. *She must've actually read the manual*, he chuckled to himself. A small gesture with his left hand activated his own signal.

"New game starting," the program announced enthusiastically as the *Big Bang* opening graphics whizzed across the players' retinas, "based on savegame scenario file *Al-814*. Please refrain from public OOC comments until the end of the game. "

"What's 'OOC'?" Go broadcast to all players.

Al winced. So did Kathy's player icon below the main game interface.

"Please refrain from public OOC comments until the end of the game," the program repeated with the exact same inflection. "God's turn starting... *now*!"

"It means 'out of character', God," Zeke explained quickly.

"Thanks, Zeke," Go said while her player icon smiled for a second.

This time, Al groaned out loud. *She knows how to use bloody emoticons, but nothing about staying in character?*

"Please," the program said with a little more emphasis than before, "refrain from public OOC comments until the end of the game."

"It's Zeus," Zeke said, "not... my other name."

"Your two minutes are already running, God! Hurry!" Al yelled after turning off his game mike. He hoped it was loud enough for Go to hear next door.

"I know, Al!" Go's high-pitched shout nearly burst the other players' eardrums. It drowned out the simultaneous external shout that Al would have heard if Go had turned off her game mike.

"Please ref—"

Al finally found the control to mute the program voice. It was the first time he had used it. *Why did I let her talk me into this?*

Go's player icon held up an apologetic hand. Even Manny's icon frowned, and he wasn't online today, replaced by a computer-controlled non-player character. Raoul was another NPC. Kathy's icon was fuming. Reluctantly, Al turned the program voice back on in case it said something useful for a change.

Then a section of the Great Sphere began to blink red to indicate that the active player was moving atoms. Al zoomed in closer to see what Go was doing. Minute and a half to go.

Yes, he nodded admiringly, *that's how you began in the practice game. Now let's see if you can adjust to a Sphere with four and a half times the mass. Bet you won't even be able to keep it stable without removing the full hundred billion you're allowed.*

"What was that about? Did you say 'God'?"

Al jumped at his mother's voice speaking so close to his left ear. He turned game vision off briefly, squeaked a quick "Mum, I'm playing!", then turned it back on. Mum always said it was impolite to speak to someone without external eye contact. *Unreal, she's fast! But... move the whole cluster, Go, not each atom separately.*

"Sorry," Al's mother said with a hint of sarcasm. "Lunch in about twenty-five minutes."

Al nodded rapidly without switching his vision to external. Did nodding count as speaking to someone? *What're you doing, Go? You're actually* adding *atoms?* Mark's player icon was scratching its head.

"Don't be late. I'll go tell Go." Mum's little joke was lost on Al, who nodded again, absently.

Then his brain registered what she'd said.

"Mum!" Internal vision off, his head whipped around, just in time before she closed the door. "I'll tell Go. Don't bother her, she's playing just now."

"Al, no. Tell me you didn't get her involved in that *Big Bang* thing."

"She asked me to show it to her. She's pretty good, you know."

"Is she?"

"Mum, gotta go back... sorry!" Internal vision came back on. If his Mum said anything else, he didn't hear it. Go's time was nearly up. Twelve seconds on the turn clock. *Whoa! What is this?*

"Ten seconds remaining," said the program.

This'll never work. Half the atoms you changed won't even affect the important part of the game. Too far away from the action, sis. I told you about that.

Bud's emoticon was laughing hysterically.

Five seconds to go. Some final moves at incredible speed, out on the Sphere's surface.

Four seconds. Nothing further happened.

Three.

Suddenly, the Sphere overview map blinked red. There was movement outside Al's currently visible area of the sphere. He zoomed out as fast as he could.

Two.

The blinking stopped, but he'd just glimpsed where the movement had been. *You can't be serious. That was halfway to the core. Way too unstable to change anything there.*

One.

Frantically, Al zoomed in to where he'd seen movement. *Dammit, what did you do there? Hey... it's actually stable. Unreal.*

Go's emoticon showed a happy smile.

"God, your time is up." The program always managed to sound remorseful when it said that. "Kali's turn starting... *now!*" You could only pick who went first; after that, it was semi-random, taking previous successes into account to make it harder for better players.

One by one, he watched the others make their moves. They mostly followed the same strategy they had always followed, with a few adjustments for Go's changes, of course. You couldn't undo another's changes. Manny tried to manipulate the area around where Go had made her last changes, resulting in loss of stability. The Sphere collapsed, and with under thirty seconds of his time to go, he was forced to start from scratch. NPCs had the same time available so that everyone could watch what they did.

When his own turn finally came, he was in his element. Once, the atoms he added threatened stability for a millisecond or two, but he was on it, adjusting, distributing and replacing at speeds that boggled the minds of the others who were watching. His sly and covert tactics would not become obvious to the others until it was too late. Every bit of experience he had earned went into his move.

Seventeen seconds to go, and he was done. He considered spending the time to see what Go had done closer to the core, but decided against it. *Let them feel their GM's superiority and confidence*, he thought as he prematurely selected the "End Turn" option.

"Contracting Sphere to Zero Density. Prepare for the *Big Bang!*"

Each player's vision turned black. Complete and utter darkness. Al loved the next part. No matter how often he saw it.

A spot of white appeared in the blackness, infinitesimally small at first, but growing at a breathtaking rate. Myriad shades of white became colours that defied belief. Then the expanding spectacle reached the players and grew larger than their internal vision could display. It overtook them, countless clusters of matter whooshed past them, and their position clamps were finally released. They were free to view the show from where they pleased.

Al surfed to where he knew the world would form, dodging the stars that were developing even as they were expelled from the centre of the universe, dodging them for the sheer fun of it. In this game, he had no substance, so anything coming his way would pass straight through him. It was great to pretend that he had to avoid things, though.

Come to think of it, much of this stuff was totally unrealistic. It was supposed to be empty space, so the sound effects were completely fabricated. And the idea of a universe expanding like this after having been contracted to Zero Density by nothing in particular was utterly preposterous. There were far more realistic games dealing with universe creation out there, but Al and his friends liked this one best. So what if the graphics were slightly outdated? Still an impressive game. The virtual universes had their own set of physical laws, albeit very limited compared to reality. But it was precisely this limitation that made the game so challenging, that kept him and the others coming back to edit the arrangement of atoms in the initial Sphere so as to improve their world each time they created it, a world that had to function despite its limitations.

Ah, there it was. Al adjusted his speed to match the forming planet's path. Game time had already begun to slow down.

And then it happened, without much fanfare at all. "Creation successful," was all the program voice said. Strange. Had that been an echo in the voice, or had Al imagined it? A link to the corresponding planet appeared in case a player didn't know where Creation had taken place. He motioned the link to go away without looking at it. As if he didn't know where it was. It had taken him weeks to achieve, weeks of meticulous study of the first two nanoseconds after the *Big Bang*, for that was when the seeds had to be planted near the Sphere's core. The closer to the core, the bigger the snowball effect. Which was why it was so astounding that Go's change had not messed it all up.

Go's icon did a little victory dance. *A bit soon for that*, he thought wryly. *I'll show you cocky after my turn. Won't underestimate you again, though. I'll let you get rid of Manny, and maybe Kathy, but if you become too big, you're gone, sis.*

Bud swooped down closer to the planet. Ever since his accidental destruction of a whole section of the world's species, which, to everyone's surprise, had actually sped up the development of the main race, he loved to watch it happen from up close. "Dino Doom", he called it.

Soon the main race set itself apart from the other developing species.

"Intelligent life found." *Definitely an echo. Might have to re-install the sound files.*

Their intelligence was increasing exponentially. It was mostly Al's doing, of course. He had designed them to appear as close to real people as he could manage. Still, they learned achingly slowly, both individually and as a race.

Game speed decreased further; things were really starting to happen. Players not already on the surface swooped down to have a closer look.

"Interaction permitted."

Nothing unusual. What the blazes were you doing, Go? As usual, first Zeke and then Mark had the largest number of followers at the early stages, increasing them by encouraging conquest. Like Raoul, generally the better of the NPCs, they also relied on portraying themselves as part of a whole group of deities. Kathy and Bud, like Manny, preferred to go solo and plant their seeds very deeply before using population explosion to drastically multiply the type of followers who were most susceptible to their wiles.

Predictably, Go had planted her own seeds of devotion in one of the areas the others largely ignored at first. *Not enough population there, they'll never amount to much. But not bad for a first try. Whoops! Sorry, sis, looks like Raoul's guys captured most of your people.*

Zeke's reign was beginning to decline, Mark was on the rise. *Almost time to interact with my believers.*

Suddenly, too quickly to make out the details, Go's people seemed to break away from Raoul's territory and rally themselves. Al glanced at Go's stats. He looked again. *What? Those stats have to be wrong!* He highlighted her territory and zoomed out a little to get a better overview. *Impossible. You can't fit that many people in that small an area. Unless....* He zoomed out even more, quickly checking every corner of the world. *Yep. Stats must be wrong.* Still, he couldn't help being a little uneasy.

Time slowed down even more.

"Entering final phase," the program said. "PMs permitted. God is in the lead with 71% of the universe's intelligent population."

A cacophony of overlapping private messages assaulted Al.

"Where *are* they?"

"Stats gotta be wrong!"

"Re-install the game, man!"

Al frantically sent PMs to each of them, but was interrupted by the program voice. "Game over for Zeus! Game over for Ra!"

Mark's people had expanded to occupy most of Go's territory, but her numbers kept growing. Then something happened that Al had never seen before.

"Is this your idea of a joke, mister GM?" Mark clamoured in Al's ear. "What did your stupid little sister do to our bloody scenario?"

With a minimum of conflict, Mark's ordinarily warlike followers were converting, turning to Go. Mark's gigantic empire was collapsing from the inside.

"Game over for Mars!" Mark's icon disappeared; he'd gone offline. *Sore loser.*

Time for Al's own strategy. One conversation with one of his followers was all there was to it.

Bud and Kathy were still growing, but nowhere near as fast as Go. The computer threw a massive plague her way; Al could see the population density in her area dropping to near zero. And yet, according to her stats, her numbers were dented only minimally for but a moment before growing again. *I don't get it... why would the numbers be wrong?*

Al's had been last up until now, but his strategy was kicking in. He was overtaking Manny, the remaining NPC, and would soon catch up to Kathy and even Bud. According to his own senses, Go wasn't far ahead of Bud, though the stats claimed otherwise. Somewhere, Mum was yelling about lunch, but he ignored her.

"Game over for Kali! Four players remaining; GB permitted."

"What the...?" Kathy said disbelievingly. Some of Go's people were controlling her area; her people turned to Bud, Al and Go. Manny's territory was already overrun with Go's invaders, his numbers fading rapidly.

"Game over for Manitou!" the program voice announced when Manny's numbers were too low to count as significant.

"Here comes the critical moment. Watch my strategy unfold, guys." The phrase had become Al's trademark over the last few hundred games.

Bud had reached a huge population, but had stopped growing at about a third of all the people on the planet. *Effectively disabled.*

"Oh look, most of the population on this side likes me," Go preened. "And over there, too. Not that it'll make a difference. Not even your nasty fanatics can make a difference, Al. Now watch *my* strategy unfold, guys."

Al was about to make a condescending reply, but then he looked at the numbers again. A terrible suspicion crept up his spine and settled carefully near the back of his skull.

Everyone was silent as they watched it happen. Al's jaw dropped onto his lap.

"Game over for Buddha! Game over for Allah! God wins the game!" The closing graphics were dazzling, underscored by the game's theme music. "Brilliant strategy, God. This scenario and its moves have been automatically submitted to the *Big Bang* prize committee for evaluation. If it's the winning entry, the last few thousand years will be run on the *Big Bang* super server at real speed so that everyone can watch the historical game unfold in every detail. Each player will be looking at a reward of—"

Al flicked the master switch.

"Uh, lunch, Go," he said into the house-internal comm.

Unreal, he thought as he headed downstairs. *Of course, the echo, the strange numbers. A second world to wipe out the first. No competition on the second one. Why didn't I think of that?*

He sat down at the lunch table, nibbled his food without really paying attention to it. A minute later, Go pranced in, giving him a cheeky smile.

"So," their mum said, joining them, "seems you did quite well for your first time, then?"

"Quite well?" Go asked. "I *showed* them how it's *done*!"

"Ah, so my little interruption worked?"

"Perfect timing, Mum," Go grinned.

Al groaned. "Yeah, you won, but you know it's just a game, right? It's not real."

"Try telling that to all those little people on my two worlds... I bet it's real to *them*." Go winked at him and scratched her left feeler absently before turning her attention to her food.

Further Stories

If you enjoyed these short stories, you may also enjoy my second collection, *Infinite Waters: 9+1 Speculative Fiction Short Stories.* You can read a short excerpt of below.

Infinite Waters: 9+1 Speculative Fiction Short Stories

What's in a Name?

"That's an unusual name for a ship."

The man facing me across the table pulled the fat cigar from his lips, leaving it to simmer inside a round ashtray. His thick brows met in the middle, as if pondering my words. Why, I could not fathom— surely, this was the single most usual comment he heard? His jowls quivered as he pushed his chair away to stand up. Hoisting his trousers up, he adjusted his life jacket and grimaced, as if in pain.

"It was a bet." With a dismissive wave of his hand, he motioned me to follow him. "A stupid bet." He sighed as he ran his fingers through thinning hair. "I lost."

That much is obvious. "Are we going somewhere?" I asked politely and grabbed my mini recorder.

"I just want to show you around. I assume your readers will want to know about the ship?"

I nodded my thanks. We weaved our way out of the smoke room and into the promenade deck. Reserved for the first-class passengers, this was not my usual kind of accommodations. My initial enthusiasm at finding out I had been sent on an assignment that allowed me to spend a week on a Caribbean cruise had waned as soon as I heard the details. The lush accommodations, however, made me rethink my initial apprehension.

The ship owner led me into the wide corridor crossing the deck. I snuck a look into a gym room, filled with ripped people in sweatpants admiring their visage in full-wall mirrors. Strangely enough, the lifejackets did not seem to bother them. A smiling blonde at the reception was handing a towel and a lifejacket to a man dressed from top to bottom in grey flannel. Splashing was heard from a wide, steel-framed door behind her. I guessed the sounds came from an indoor swimming pool. Judging by the steam on the glass, the doors next to it led to a spa or sauna. My muscles ached for a massage, but that would have to wait. I was here for a job.

"Do they wear lifejackets in the pool?" I wondered aloud.

"Everyone has to wear their lifejacket twenty-four-seven. It's part of the insurance policy." For the first time since we met, the foreboding cloud lifted from his eyes and the man grinned. "It gives them something to tell their friends after the cruise."

"Is the name also why you only do Caribbean cruises?"

"Can't be too careful," the man agreed.

I stepped aside as a slender girl rushed out a door and almost crashed into us. She was balancing half a dozen books, taken from what I guessed was the lending library. With a shy smile, she dashed down the corridor and into the reading room. Her lifejacket bounced against the doorframe, almost making her drop the books, but she managed to hold on to them at the last moment.

"Are you coming?"

Despite his short stature and rotund figure, the ship owner could move fast. I hurried up after him, my eye catching on the Renaissance-style trimmings. The impression was of a floating five-star hotel rather than a ship. All first-class common rooms were adorned with ornate wood paneling and expensive furniture.

We passed an open door leading to the outside deck. In the morning, this would be filled with a throng of passengers socializing, promenading or relaxing in hired deck chairs and sculpted wooden benches. Now, however, it lay empty. I stole a look outside. It was a brilliant, starry night. With no moon to mar the sky, the stars sparkled bright. I had never seen a smoother sea; it was like a quiet pond, and just as innocent looking, as the great ship quietly rippled through it. I half-expected a flock of wild geese to land any moment.

Someone closed the door and passed me by, snapping me back to the present. I followed the ship owner down the Grand Staircase, one of the most distinctive features of the ship. It descended through seven decks. A dome of wrought iron and glass capping it admitted natural light in the morning, although it now lay dark, like a black, polished diamond. A large, carved wooden panel above us contained a clock, with figures of "Honor and Glory crowning Time" flanking the clock face. I could not help but gape at the beauty of it all.

Upon reaching the landing, we entered an ornate hall lit by gold-plated light fixtures. Well-laid tables filled the room. White linen covered the tops. Silver cutlery clanked against porcelain dishes.

Waiters meandered skillfully to serve dinner to hungry first-class passengers.

Music came from the far end, obscuring the diners' soft murmur. I recognized "O mio Babbino Caro" and half-expected to hear a soprano—maybe even Callas herself, brought back from the dead—singing the aria. "The Café Parisien offers the best French haute cuisine for first-class passengers," the man said with a well-practiced flourish.

"And the music?"

"Our very own small *ensemble*. Eight musicians, the very best."

"They'd have to be, to play with their lifejackets on," I could not help but joke.

He did not seem to share my mirth, and muttered something under his breath. He spun around to continue the tour, when a jolt reverberated through the hull. It was so strong that it knocked me off my feet, sending me to land on my lifejacket. A mannequin crashed through a glass display and dropped next to me. *I survived a cruise on...* , the t-shirt it wore read. The rest of the inscription was obscured by the doll's broken arm.

I heard shouts all around me. Angry claxons blared in alarm. People clamored. Lights dimmed, and shone again. Then, it all stopped. An eerie silence fell. Dazed people struggled to get their bearings. Expensive leather shoes and elegant high heels stepped on salmon and pheasant as stunned diners rose to their feet. Fear and silent pleas for help filled the passengers' eyes. I turned to the ship owner, but he had disappeared. From afar, I heard one long continuous wailing chant, like locusts on a midsummer night in the woods. *Have people jumped overboard?* I decided to follow the noise. The flickering lights allowed me to reach the nearest exit, pushing through the nervous throng.

I had just reached the door handle when the floor tilted. The vessel reared up, followed by a rumbling roar and a muffled explosion. I pushed through the door and grabbed the railing. For a moment, all that I could hear was the keening of the wind in the halyards and the wash of the sea against the ship's hull. Then, the ship let out a terrible groan and quivered, like a mongrel trying to throw the fleas off its back. I hesitated but for a second, then hauled myself over the railing and jumped.

After a heart-stopping moment of weightlessness, I crashed into the sea. I was pushed out at first, then sucked down. The water was warm, but the shock took the breath out of my lungs. Down and down I went, spinning around like a lost sock in a washing machine. I swam as hard as I could in the direction which I thought to be the surface. With no sun or moon to show me the way, I had to guess. My heart beat so fast, I thought it would pop out of my chest. Finally, it occurred to me to let my lifejacket guide me to the surface. Just before my lungs burst, I came up.

I drank the night air with deep, thirsty gulps. Falling debris dragged me underwater again. Kicking my feet, I fought back to the surface. With a loud splash, I came up against a lifeboat. Too exhausted to haul myself, I let the men already inside pull me up.

I landed on the fiberglass floor and splashed in the shallow water there. It stunk of engine oil, petrol and sea water. The sweetest smell to ever hit my nostrils. Someone helped me to my feet and sat me down. I nodded my thanks and coughed to clear my lungs. Salt burned my eyes and my throat.

"Are you all right?"

Recognizing the voice, I looked up and saw the ship owner. "I will be, thanks," I rasped after a moment. I drew a deep breath, grateful to be alive. "What the hell happened?"

"A ship collided with us," the man said. "Those idiots must have been drunk or something."

I shook my head. I had heard stories of crews drinking on the job, but this was one for the books. The huge cruise ship was not exactly hard to miss.

I glanced outside. Cut in half, our ship had capsized and was about to go under. A second ship tilted drunkenly next to it. In the dark, it was hard to make out, but it looked like a freighter.

My eye caught on something like countless heads bobbing on the water. "My God," I whispered. "Are those people?"

The man leaned next to me and craned his head to look. "No, that's not heads." He looked forlorn. "It's lettuce. That damn ship was filled with it." His eyes glinted with something akin to madness. "We were struck by a freighter carrying iceberg lettuce."

"Iceberg lett—" I coughed to swallow the mad cackle that rose to my throat, shaking my head. "Buddy, *that's* why you don't call your ship the Titanic II."

A Note from the Author

These short stories were written between July 2009 and March 2012. Shortly afterwards, I started work on my first novel, *Pearseus.* Although they seem to be concerned with various themes, there are certain passions that run through them, almost obsessively. What is the nature of reality? Is there more to the world than we can see?

The first story, "Simulation Over," is based on a dream I had, and deals with Descartes' age-old question; how far can we trust our senses? With technology progressing rapidly, the time can't be far off when it will be practically impossible to tell apart sensory fact from simulation. How will we be able to tell fantasy and reality apart? The story was published by *magazine 9* on October 17th, 2009.

The second story, "For the Last Time," is lighter in nature. Another common theme, explored in depth in *Pearseus,* is that of the choices we make and their consequences. The main character here makes one mistake after another. As a result, he keeps getting in deeper and deeper trouble, until he realizes how happy he was before all this. As the saying goes, "I'd like to be who I was before I became who I am".

The inspiration for the third story, "The Hand of God," came while playing Starcraft™ (and getting pounded time after time in that final level). It deals with that old question of the nature of reality – digital and corporeal. What do the game characters do when we stop playing?

The fourth story, "I Come in Peace" (from the common sci-fi first contact words), deals with a tortuous question: how far would man go to alleviate his loneliness? In particular, a man experiencing what is possibly the worst kind of loneliness; that someone feels when surrounded by people?

This story explores this basic human emotion – the need for companionship. It won the SF competition titled *Invasion* and was published by *Cube Publishing* in the anthology of the same name. Readers of *Pearseus* will certainly recognise here the birth of the Orbs.

The fifth story, "A Fresh Start," is, again, about choices – and a favourite question: if we were free to go anywhere in time and space, where would we choose to go? And, once there, would we repeat the same mistakes, or make new ones? What does a man really need to be happy?

The sixth story, "The Sentry," was inspired by Philip K. Dick's first story, *Roog*. Science fiction fans will surely recognize this nod to the old master.

The final story, "Big Bang," is written by my author friend, **Amos M. Carpenter**. Amos lives in Australia, I live in Greece. We've never met in person. And yet, his story is written in a style eerily similar to mine; as such, it is a great complement to the rest in the book. You can find out more about Amos and his work on his blog, amosmcarpenter.com

One common characteristic of all stories is a disdain for names, both for characters and places. This is because of my conviction that names inevitably restrict the reader's imagination. We all carry deep in our psyche an image for all names and places and this will necessarily carry on to the story, limiting the possible projections we can perform. I'd rather leave the canvas completely blank, so that readers can colour it any way they like.

About the Author

Nicholas Rossis lives to write and does so from his cottage on the edge of a magical forest in Athens, Greece. When not composing epic fantasies or short sci-fi stories, he chats with fans and colleagues, writes blog posts, walks his dog, and enjoys the antics of two silly cats,  one of whom claims his lap as home. His children's book, Runaway Smile, earned a finalist slot in the 2015 International Book Awards.

Nicholas is all around the Internet, but the best place to connect with him would be on his blog, http://nicholasrossis.me/

Anyone interested in his books can check them out on Amazon:

http://www.amazon.com/Nicholas-C.-Rossis/e/B00FXXIBZA/

People can read *Runaway Smile* for free on http://nicholasrossis.me/childrens-books/

Acknowledgments

They say that everyone has a book in them. What they don't say is how much it helps if you're not alone in your journey to share your words with the world.

Many thanks to <u>Amos M. Carpenter</u> for allowing me to include his wonderful story here; my excellent editor, <u>Lorelei Logsdon</u>; and everyone who helped with their feedback, namely <u>The Story Reading Ape</u>, <u>sallyember</u>, <u>M T McGuire</u>, <u>kanzensakura</u>, <u>Michelle Proulx</u>, <u>TheCrazyBagLady</u> and Karen. Special thanks to George Giaglis, my very first beta-reader. Also, to my wonderful friends and beta-readers <u>Dormaine G</u>, Elpida Arslanoglou, <u>MMJaye</u>, <u>Effrosyni Moschoudi</u>, <u>Elle Boca</u>, Alisson Karr, <u>Danica Cornell</u>, <u>Nat Russo</u>, <u>Wendy Ewurum</u> and my fiercest critic and greatest help, my wife Electra.

Yes, all these wonderful people helped out. It takes a village, as they say, and without them, this journey would have been much poorer.

Further Notes

If you enjoyed *The Power of Six*, continue reading with
Infinite Waters, now available on Amazon:

http://amzn.to/1IpsEC5

Want to contact me? Eager for an e-book autograph?
Follow me on http://nicholasrossis.me

For every new follower,

my dog does a happy dance... :)

If you wish to report a typo or have reviewed this book on Amazon,
please email *info@nicholasrossis.com* with the word "review" on the
subject line, to receive a free 1680x1050 Pearseus desktop
background.

Thank you for taking the time to read The Power of Six! If you enjoyed it, please consider telling your friends or posting a short review. Word of mouth is an author's best friend and much appreciated.

This is an original work of fiction. Any relationship to real people is unintentional and a coincidence.

Made in the USA
Coppell, TX
16 March 2022